Chapter 1: The Morning After

Juliette woke up, naked, in a strange bed. That was never a good sign.

A hand was draped loosely across her waist and the steady deep breaths of sleeping filled the room. Juliette glanced at Mr. Blue Eyes and noted she was not the only one lacking clothes.

Terrence's skin was rich and buttery, his chest smooth and bare. Her eyes trailed over his well-toned, rock-hard stomach and quivered at the memory of their bodies pressed together. Juliette longed to reach out to him, to pull him close and greet him with a little morning romp. But the heavy pounding on the door broke through her thoughts.

"Yo, T!" a man's voice yelled. "Come on man, open up. You're late."

Juliette sprang from the bed and grabbed the sheets to cover her bare chest. She could hear the doorknob jingle followed by a soft beep of a key card being rejected. Did this guy have a key? Was he going to come in and find her here, naked in Terrence's hotel suite?

Terrence grumbled something incoherent into the pillow. He didn't look anywhere near waking up.

Juliette climbed out of bed, dragging the top sheet off the mattress, and made a mad dash for the bathroom. Only the bathroom turned out to be a closet. Clenching the oversized sheet tight around her body, she searched the room for her clothes: bra, panties, skirt, blouse, and heels. It was challenging to say the least. She finally gathered all her belongings and made her way into the main room, just as the door to the suite opened and an Asian man in his mid-twenties stepped inside.

Juliette froze. There were two closed doors on the other side of the sitting room. One of them was bound to be a bathroom. Of course, the only way she could get to them was to sprint across the suite, right past the kitchenette and Terrence's new guest.

"Come on, T! What the hell, man? Get up." He moved farther into the room, letting the door close behind him, and tossed his keycard on the counter. He still hadn't spotted her. Maybe she could make it back to the bedroom.

Nope. Too late. The man was headed right for her. Juliette attempted to run but her feet got caught up in the bed sheets.

"Oh, hi," he said.

She gave a slight wave then clutched the sheet tighter. "Hello."

"So you're the reason my guy is late."

"Sorry," she said. "I was just getting ready to leave."

"Right. Well, bathroom is that way," he said and pointed across the room.

Juliette took the exit option and shuffled across the room. She dressed as quickly as possible and then made a desperate attempt to clean herself up. She wasn't about to use a stranger's toothbrush, even if they had gotten up-close and personal the night before. Instead, Juliette reached for the bottle of mouthwash and took a swig. The minty plaque remover would have to do. She washed her face and then pulled her hair into a loose braid. There. It wasn't perfect, but she might not be picked out of the walk-of-shame lineup.

Juliette counted to three and pulled the door open. Terrence and the new guy were huddled around the counter. Terrence had managed to put on a pair of boxers, but that wasn't enough coverage to make her forget about the night's naughty activities.

"Your phone keeps beeping." The Asian guy with the spiked hair tossed a cell phone in her direction. Juliette caught it in her left hand. *Thank God for quick reflexes.*

"Oh my God." Juliette stared in amazement at the blue and white text message overlaying her flowered screensaver and couldn't believe her eyes. It was a text message from Dean Covington. It was so short and simple.

You've got the job. 1776 K Street NW 9 a.m.

Juliette glanced at her watch. It was a quarter to nine now.

"Shit!"

The two men were now staring at her.

"Is something wrong?" Terrence asked.

"I got the job!" Juliette grinned before practically skipping over to Terrence and kissing him on the cheek. "I got the job."

"Congratulations." He gave her a tight squeeze.

"I have to go."

"Right now?"

"Yeah. I'm supposed to be there in less than fifteen minutes."

He took a closer look at her. "If that's the case, you might want to wear a clean shirt."

Juliette looked down at the white blouse. "I don't have time to change."

But Terrence wasn't listening. He disappeared into the bedroom and came out with a gray button-down shirt. "It'll be a little big, but I think you can pull it off. Just roll up the sleeves or something."

The other guy stared at him. "Did I go to sleep and wake up on *Project Runway*?"

"Hey, don't hate on me because I know something about fashion."

Juliette dropped her phone and purse on the counter, pulled the day-old blouse over her head, and grabbed the shirt from Terrence.

"Stop staring," she warned, and Terrence and the unnamed guy spun away. Terrence was right. If she rolled the sleeves up, left the last three buttons undone, and tied the ends into an eighties-style knot, she almost looked trendy.

"See, perfect," Terrence said when she allowed them to turn around again.

"Yeah, oddly sexy." The other guy agreed. But Juliette was no longer listening. She picked up her bag and the worn shirt and made a beeline for the door.

Chapter 2: The Drop Off

Juliette wasn't certain what to expect as she stood at the corner of K Street and Connecticut Avenue. Was Covington going to magically appear and give her the details of her new assignment?

No. Nico Bertoletti, one of Dean's thugs, stopped in front of her and held out a manila folder. Nico was a big Italian guy with short graying hair and a handful of scars that lined the side of his face. When Dean didn't want to get his hands dirty, Nico stepped in. If she remembered correctly, torture was his specialty. He was dressed in business attire: black suit, black leather jacket, black suede shoes. Not the attire she's d expect if he were here to bring her harm.

"What is this?" She asked, feeling a little 007.

Nico smirked. "If you have to ask maybe you shouldn't be in this line of work."

Juliette studied the folder. It wasn't a thick file, probably only a dozen or so pages inside. She flipped the top cover open and Nico clenched his hand around it, clamping the pages shut. "Not here."

"Then where?"

"I don't care." He shoved the folder at her. "Just not here."

Nico shook his head and grumbled something incomprehensible before he turned and disappeared into the crowd.

"Thanks for your help." Juliette shoved the file folder into her purse and headed for the metro. As the escalator glided deep into the underground belly of D.C. Juliette felt the folder calling out to her. What did Covington have in store for her--stealing art like her parents, or perhaps impersonating a buyer?

Juliette followed the crowd of travelers to the subway platform. When the tourists stopped right at the foot of the stairs she pushed forward, headed for the less deserted section. She leaned against the cement column and reached for her bag. Now that Nico was out of sight she could examine the contents in peace. Inside there was a four-by-six picture of a young woman with blonde hair, blue eyes, and the perfect California tan. Her name was Courtney Anderson. Her father was Governor Davis Anderson. She was a third-year law student at George Washington University, the editor of the school's law review, and captain of the crew team. *Where in the world did this girl find time for crew?*

Juliette skimmed the rest of the memo, her eyes landing on a highlighted sentence in the last paragraph about a campaign rally at McPherson Square on August 25th. She glanced down at her cell phone.

Great. That was today. Looked like she was going to have to jump right in with a little morning recon. No wonder Covington had wanted her so damn early.

McPherson was only a few blocks away--in the opposite direction.

Juliette whipped the folder closed and headed back to the stairs. If she could get to the other side of the platform before the next train arrived she could hop off at the next stop and be right at the park. She huffed up each step, darted between a handful of tourists, and made her way across the bridge. A tone sounded, alerting the arrival of an oncoming train-- her train. Juliette picked up the pace, as did a few other regular commuters around her. Together they ambled down the escalator and onto the already overcrowded platform.

The train screeched to a stop just as she reached the second car door. The doors trudged open and the crowd filed in. Inside it was hot and smelled like sweat. The air conditioner was either turned off or broken. Good thing her ride was short.

Juliette braced herself against the metal arm-rail as the train began to move. She turned her attention back to the file folder and began to study the rest of the contents. There was a copy of an article about the governor of Virginia. Apparently he was a big shot and more than one political pundit expected that he might run for the presidency in 2016.

Juliette glanced back at the picture of the girl.

So was Anderson the real target?

She flipped the next page and got her answer. It was a GWU Fall Semester class schedule for Courtney with a sticky note attached. The note read: *Become Courtney's best friend and await further instructions.*

The brevity of the note was all Covington. One line, nothing else. No mention of why or how. No mention of the bigger job at stake, and there was most definitely a bigger job on the line. *What use would Covington have with a college coed?*

A tone rang out and the train driver mumbled something garbled into the intercom about the next stop. How tourists managed to get around using the metro when conductors barely spoke a coherent word into the microphone was beyond her.

Juliette shoved the papers back into her bag and moved toward the sliding doors. When the train came to a stop and the doors slid open she was the first one onto the platform. She used her New York City walk to brush past the casual onlookers and slightly weary travelers who were already dreading the heat of the hot August summer. She bypassed the tourists, took the middle of the three escalators, and trudged up the left side with the other overeager pedestrians--who used the hike as a good excuse to skip the gym.

When the escalator stairs curled around the sidewalk and leveled out with the pavement Juliette stepped out into the welcome sunshine. She spotted her destination immediately. It was hard to miss, actually, with the red, white, and blue balloon arch that spanned over the lower entrance to McPherson Square. A large banner hung a foot beneath the highest point in the arch and it read, "Tyler Chase for U.S. Senator". The name was unfamiliar. The photo beneath it was not. The brown curls, the dimpled smile, and those godforsaken blue eyes.

Chapter 3: Meet the Mark

Juliette stared back at those familiar blue eyes. There had to be some explanation. Tyler Chase was a U.S. Senator, running for re-election in November. The man she had slept with was a bike messenger named Terrence.

Her stomach clenched. She never asked him what he did for a living; she just assumed he was a bike messenger or intern because of his dress. And he was way too young and dreamy to be a politician. She couldn't remember the last time she saw any politician on the national stage who wasn't well into their forties or fifties. And Terrence--well, Tyler, she supposed she should use his real name--looked at least a decade away from hitting the big four-oh.

There had to be an explanation, she argued with herself again.

Well of course there was. She was drunk, he was horny. They did what drunk and horny people do--

lied to each other and had hot sweaty sex on the kitchen counter.

She wanted to be mad at him for keeping his true identity a secret. But then again she hadn't been completely forthright about her identity either. Who was she to get her panties all twisted up in a bunch?

The more she thought about Tyler--with his smooth smile, charming words, and the ability to completely woo her back to his apartment within a matter of hours--the more certain she was. Tyler Chase was either a politician or a crook. They were really one in the same.

Juliette was half tempted to skip the event altogether. But then she remembered the real reason she had come to the park. She was supposed to be looking for her mark, Courtney Anderson. She must have been attending the event with the governor.

One deep breath and a few shoulder rolls later, Juliette was pumped up and ready to go. She stepped under the sea of balloons and entered the world of politics.

Before she could even scan the area a handful of volunteers accosted her. "Vote for Chase," two blonde sorority girls said as they thrust a stack of stickers and postcards her way. Juliette took the swag without thinking and shoved it into her bag as she continued on with the crowd. The last thing she needed was another reminder of her one-night stand.

The event appeared to be well underway. There was a makeshift stage to the right of the McPherson statue where a podium, more balloons, and several men in dark suits had gathered. To the left of the stage, standing near some not-so-safe looking stairs, was her girl. Courtney Anderson looked every bit the part of a politician's daughter. She could have been plucked right out of a Ralph Lauren ad in her sheer Carolina blue blouse, cream slacks, and navy flats. Her hair was knotted up in a loose bun. If she had a rebellious streak, she hid it well. There was no sign of a party girl in her past, present, or future.

Great. Getting to know this girl was going to be loads of fun.

Courtney turned and stepped into a crowd of guests. Juliette kept her distance, choosing instead to let the girl come to her. That meant Juliette needed to blend in. Everyone else seemed to be toting around water bottles with red and white "Chase for Change" labels. So she made her way to the coolers. They were also red, white, and blue. *Because any other color might be unpatriotic.* She reached into the cooler and flinched at the ice-cold water.

Another person reached in after her. "Crap, that's cold," he said, and Juliette looked up.

Crap was right.

She was standing next to the mystery man who witnessed her naked bout around the senator's hotel suite. *Could this day get any more awkward?*

His eyes grew wide when he recognized her. "What are you doing here?"

"Me? I'm attending a political rally for class," she lied. "Clearly I don't have to ask what you're doing here." She gave a nod to the Tyler Chase sticker on his t-shirt.

"That's right, we weren't properly introduced this morning." He gave her a knowing smile as if she was supposed to be proud of the senator's late-night conquest and her early-morning walk of shame. "I'm Winston. Senator Chase's campaign manager."

Juliette frowned. He didn't look like a Winston. And though he was dressed in dark pants and wore a Tyler Chase t-shirt over his much nicer button-down shirt, he didn't look like any campaign manager she had ever met.

"Is he here?" Juliette asked and then instantly felt like a moron.

Winston smirked at her. "Of course he's here. This is his event."

Crap, crap, crap. What the hell are you doing, Juliette?

"Look, we need all the votes we can get, but I'm not sure your being here is wise."

"Oh, so sleeping around with young coeds is not part of Mr. Chase's platform?"

Winston nearly choked on his water. "No, it's not. I'm afraid you just caught him at an off moment."

"Right."

Suddenly her mouth was a bit too dry. Juliette twisted the cap off her own bottle of water and took a swig. "You don't have to worry. I'll keep my mouth shut."

Winston didn't look convinced, but Juliette wasn't prepared to stand there all day and reassure him.

"I'd like to believe you, but I can't afford to take you at your word."

What did he want, a signed confidentiality statement?

Winston reached into his pocket and pulled out a folded-up envelope. Juliette's jaw scraped the ground. "Please tell me you're not trying to pay me off."

"Why? Can your silence be bought?"

"No."

Winston opened the envelope. "You should sign this."

"Excuse me?" *Did the guy really carry around confidentiality statements? How many girls could*

Chase have slept with that he had the legal documents on hand?

"Relax," he said. "Just a precaution. It basically says that you won't speak to the press about the senator or matters of the campaign without our express permission."

"Why would I speak to the press?"

He gave her a wary look.

"Right," she said and took the paper from him. "How about I have my lawyer look over this and get back to you?"

Winston looked as if he wanted to argue more, but she didn't give him the chance. Juliette turned and ran right smack into her mark.

Courtney smiled at Winston, immediately spotting the folded envelope in his hand. "Don't tell me you've got another new volunteer lined up," she said to Winston.

"What can I say, Tyler loves the college vote."

Winston gave Juliette one last look before backing off into the crowd.

"Ignore him," Courtney said. "He's well on his way to joining the cynical and bitter politicians roaming the streets of D.C."

Courtney extended her manicured hand. "We're glad you could make it out today."

"Thanks." Juliette shook the girl's hand. Her grip was surprisingly firm and confident.

Something darkened on Courtney's face. "Oh, my." Her voice became throaty. "You seem to be missing a Chase for Change sticker" She reached into her pocket and produced a handful of the large blue and white circles. Before Juliette could stop her, Courtney peeled away the back and placed the sticker on her chest, patting it a few times to be sure it stuck.

"What a nice shirt," she said. "I could swear I've seen one just like it."

Juliette shrugged, distracted as her gaze slipped over to the stage. "I borrowed it from my roommate this morning. I spilled syrup on mine at breakfast."

She tried to force her eyes back to Courtney but it was impossible. Tyler Chase was on the stairs of the stage, staring back at her. She couldn't tell if he was happy or terrified to see her. Then Winston leaned over his shoulder and whispered something into his ear. The reminder of the confidentiality statement was enough to make her nauseous. She tore her eyes away from Ty and focused her attention on Courtney, who was going on about difficult stains.

Courtney looked up on stage. "Oh it looks like we're ready to start. Don't forget to tell your friends to vote Chase."

Juliette watched as Courtney made her way to the stage, pausing to shake hands with a few supporters and volunteers as she passed by. At the foot of the steps Governor Anderson pulled her close and kissed her on the cheek. He made his way past Ty, but not before patting him on the back and wishing him luck.

The crowd cheered as Anderson made his way to the podium, but it wasn't the governor Juliette was interested in. Courtney climbed the remaining stairs to stand directly behind Ty. She placed both her hands on his shoulders and then gave him a chaste kiss on the cheek. Her mouth lingered near his neck as she whispered something into his ear. Most of the crowd had probably missed it, but Juliette couldn't look away. Not with Tyler Chase staring right at her.

Chapter 4:

The Candidate Surprise

Even after Courtney pulled away from the embrace, Juliette couldn't take her eyes off the stage. Governor Anderson called out to Tyler. The crowd erupted into cheers. Tyler gave her one last longing look before turning to the rest of the crowd and lighting up the stage with that killer smile.

The noise of the crowd was the perfect distraction. Without his gaze beating down on her, Juliette was once again able to think straight. And everything inside her was screaming to run now. Fast. Nothing good was going to come if she stayed here pining for Tyler Chase. And more importantly, if she wasn't careful, she would ruin her chance at getting close to Courtney and thus winning over Covington enough to join his inner circle.

Juliette backed away, tossing the bottle of water in the first trash bin she saw. It landed with a hard thud. She imagined whopping Tyler over the head with the same force. But the memory of those piercing eyes and sweet lips coming down on hers

Crap. She was so completely screwed.

"Hey," a voice called out to her.

Juliette looked up. Winston was standing a few feet away. He raised his arms in a surrendering gesture when he saw the fury in her eyes. "You okay?"

"Of course I'm okay," Juliette spat. "I'm not some silly girl who falls to pieces because she had an unfortunate run-in with some lying, cheating dick-wad."

Winston took a step backward. "Hey, that dick-wad you're referring to is a U.S. Senator. Have a little respect."

"Excuse me?"

"Come on. You really expect me to believe that you had no idea who he was? Didn't you think it odd when he brought you back to a hotel room? That probably should have been your first clue."

"Clearly I was off my game," Juliette snapped.

"Right. Well don't pin all the blame on Terrence. I doubt he expected to see you again."

"Did you just call him Terrence? What is that? His 'I wanna get dirty code name?'"

For the first time since this morning Winston looked flustered.

Juliette barely choked down a bitter laugh. "You aren't just his campaign manager, are you?"

"Tyler Chase is a good friend." He stressed the name Tyler.

"Yeah, well your friend is an ass."

He nodded, not bothering to argue.

"Does he do this often? Sleep with random women?"

Winston shook his head. "He's a good man."

"And what about Courtney? How does she fit in?"

"Her father is important. The governor single-handedly launched Tyler's political career. He appointed him to fill the vacant Senate seat after Senator Reis's death. His endorsement not only gets him political cred, but generates hundreds of thousands of dollars in campaign contributions."

"So are you telling me that the thing with Courtney is all an act to appease her father?"

"No." Winston took a few steps closer. "I think they care about each other. I hope they do." He hesitated as if doubting his next words but in the end trudged on. "Don't take this the wrong way, but no one wins if you go public. Courtney will get hurt. Ty will lose the election. And despite what you might think about him, he's done amazing things for the state of Virginia."

Jules didn't want to agree with Winston, but she did. Nothing good could come out of spilling her secret with the world. She needed to be friends with Courtney, not sworn enemies. The only way to do that was to forget about Ty. To act as though the other night had never happened. And to start over.

"I'll keep his secret," Juliette said and pulled out the confidentiality statement. She reached into her purse, took out a pen, and then scrawled her signature at the bottom without a further glance at the statement above. "You can have this back. If it makes you feel better."

He hesitated before taking the paper and tucking it back into his pocket. "You're doing the right thing."

"Trust me. I don't need you to tell me that."

Winston headed back toward the rally. Juliette leaned back against the tree and watched him go. She should leave too. There was nothing more she could do here. But she wasn't ready to leave yet. Juliette glanced down at her shirt, *Ty's* shirt, and pulled off the Chase for Change sticker. There was no point dreaming about the impossible. Tyler Chase was not hers to have. Her energies were better focused on finding the truth about her parents' murder. And that meant doing a perfect job for Dean Covington.

Chapter 5: Keeping Secrets

The apartment had an empty feeling to it when Juliette arrived. Her roommate, Margaret, was on a two-month internship in New Mexico studying Native American Art on the Mescalero Apache Reservation. It was odd not having Margaret around. She had a chatty personality that always filled the place with laughter and warmth. Without her it felt like a doctor's waiting room. Cold and sterile.

Juliette curled up on the sofa and clicked on the TV. She had already ditched her twice-worn clothes in the hamper--where she seriously considered burning Ty's gray shirt--and taken a nice, hot shower. Now that she was clean and wearing her baggy yoga pants and a long-sleeved tee, she felt a little less like Jules Everdeen, the strung out art history graduate with a crazy mission to befriend Governor Anderson's daughter, and more like Juliette Morgan, the orphaned kid from Brooklyn. Then she popped in a copy of *Rocky*, father's favorite movie, and her transition was complete.

After the movie she decided to do her own research on Tyler Chase and Courtney Anderson. She needed to find a way into Courtney's everyday life--hopefully one that didn't involve Tyler. She pulled out her laptop and waited for the search engine to load. She had just typed in Governor Anderson's name when her cell phone rang.

Jules reached for the phone and scanned the caller ID. She recognized the number immediately. It was her godparents, Mimi and Jean.

"Hello."

"Oh, so you do still know our number," Mimi cooed into the phone. "I was starting to think you forgot it."

"Never," she said to her godmother. "I've just been busy with all the post-graduation stuff."

"You mean all the Dean Covington stuff?"

"What?"

"Don't lie to me, Juliette. I know you had your job interview with Dean Covington yesterday."

How could she possibly know that?

"You know how we feel about that man. He's no good."

"Yes, yes. You've said as much before."

"And yet you don't seem to be listening."

Juliette sighed. "I hear you. I just don't agree with you. And whatever you said to Covington to keep him from hiring me didn't work."

Mimi went silent on the other end of the line. "What do you mean?"

"He hired me today. I've already got my first assignment."

"Jewel." Her godmother used her favorite nickname in that warning tone.

"It's okay. You don't have to be happy for me."

"It's not that. I just don't want to see you get hurt. Dean Covington is a dangerous man."

"You don't think I know that? My parents are dead because of him. And who knows how many other innocent people he's taken down."

"And what do you expect to do? The man has almost as many friends as he does enemies. No one on either side of the law has been able to take him down."

"I'm not trying to take him down. I just want to know the truth. I deserve to know who betrayed my parents. They died doing his dirty work and I want to know why."

"Juliette. Let it go. You are young and alive and have the whole world at your beck and call. Don't waste precious time chasing Dean Covington's web of lies."

There was a soft rapping at her door.

"Someone's at the door. I have to go." She caught Mimi's soft 'I love you's just before she said goodbye. She knew her godmother was upset. Mimi couldn't understand why Juliette wouldn't just let it go and embrace the life she and Jean had provided for her. It wasn't that she didn't love them like parents, or didn't appreciate everything they did. She was lucky she had two amazing people to take her in. She just couldn't live with the fact that her parents were dead and a guy like Dean Covington was not.

Juliette pulled herself up from the couch and shuffled over to the door, still wrapped in the checkered throw from the couch. There was a chill in the air she hadn't noticed earlier and she didn't want to let go of the warmth of the blanket.

She pulled open the door without thinking and stared into the hallway at Tyler Chase. Ugh, she should have checked the peephole. At least then she would have been prepared for what awaited her.

"Hey, Jules."

Of all the questions she could have asked the one that surfaced to the top would have made Jean and Mimi proud. "How the hell did you get my address?"

Ty grinned and stretched all six feet of his long, lean figure across the door frame. He tilted his head to the side. "I have super powers."

She wanted to roll her eyes and laugh, but had a feeling that would only encourage further misbehavior. And she didn't want Ty to think it was okay that he just showed up at her apartment. Normal people don't do that kind of thing. Stalkers maybe. Or crooks. Or politicians who wanted to hide any evidence of a sex scandal.

Focus, Juliette. A strange man just showed up at your door.

"I'm serious," Juliette tried again. "How did you get my address?"

Tyler gave a shrug. "Winston."

Juliette threw her hands into the air. "Who is that guy? And don't tell me he's your campaign manager."

"Is that what he told you?"

"Yes. But I don't believe him. Nor do I believe that his real name is Winston."

"Why, because he's Korean? He was born and raised in Beverly Hills. He's lucky his name is not Apple."

L.A., huh? That explained his impeccable fashion sense. She wondered if this Boy Wonder also dressed his supposed boss. There's no way Ty picked out the dark jeans and blazer he was now sporting. Absolutely no way.

"Is he gay?" Juliette asked without thinking.

"Not everyone in L.A. is gay."

Juliette sighed. "That's not what I meant. I'm not homophobic or anything. I just noticed he has amazing fashion sense."

Ty rubbed his hands over the front of his jeans. "Yeah, he taught me everything he knows."

"I hope not everything." Juliette couldn't help herself.

"Ahh, so you did have a good time last night."

The image of the two of them together in his hotel suite, him pressed up against her in a hallway very much like the one they were standing in now, was too much to bear. She wasn't supposed to be standing here, flirting with him. *He is a U.S senator. With a girlfriend.*

"I think you should leave now."

Ty frowned at the abrupt transition. "I'd rather come in."

"Never going to happen."

"I just want a chance to explain what happened this morning, with Courtney."

The name slammed into her like a defensive lineman. She cringed at the thought of what Courtney might think if she learned the truth about Juliette and Ty.

"There's nothing to talk about. You're dating Courtney. She seems nice. You should spend more time visiting her and less time here with me."

"It's not like that."

"I don't care," Juliette snapped. "What happened last night was a one-time thing. I was having an off day and needed a distraction to cheer me up. Now I'm better and I can take it from here, thank you very much."

She didn't wait for Ty to say more. She simply stepped backward and closed the door. After it clicked shut she leaned against the cold metal and listened for Ty's footsteps on the other side. Was he still there, or had he taken the hint and left? How long did she have to wait before she could check?

No, she told herself. There will be no checking. She had more important things to do and hooking up with a U.S. senator was not one of them.

Chapter 6: The Keating Five

Juliette studied her mark at a distance for two whole days before making her next move. Courtney, it seemed, was like fire and ice all rolled up into one. If there was something she wanted, she generally got it. And she wasn't shy about making her opinions known. What worried Juliette more was Courtney's WASP-like demeanor. The girl lived her life like a giant chess match, always thinking three steps ahead. She stockpiled political ammo like others collected baseball cards and waited undeterred for the most opportune time to make her move. It was how she dethroned her undergrad class president and how she managed to secure the position as editor of the law review. Courtney wasn't smarter than those in her law school class, she was just more devious.

Which was why Juliette wound up in the law library, holding a stack of legal research briefs with a perplexed expression on her face. She needed the public setting for their first encounter and the quiet nature of the library practically guaranteed Courtney wouldn't be able to make a scene.

Juliette clutched the carefully selected papers to her chest as if she were carrying illegal contraband. She moved between the study carrels where Courtney was hard at work and deliberately tripped on the back of her chair leg.

"What the hell?" Courtney snapped as her chair jerked backward and the legal briefs Juliette had been carrying scattered into the air. Juliette clutched the edge of the table to regain her balance. The tips of her fingers brushed the back of Courtney's hand. Then she let out a pathetic whine as she fell to the floor.

Everyone in the room froze. A few heads poked out of the cubbies to see what all the commotion was about. Courtney glowered down at her. Juliette had seen that expression before. It was a mixture of anger, annoyance, and loathing. She expected Courtney to say something snarky, like, "Walk much?" or, "Maybe if you didn't buy cheap knock-off shoes, you wouldn't trip over your own two feet." But her irritation evaporated the moment she realized the other law students watching them.

"I'm so sorry," Juliette said. "I don't know what happened. I was just trying to find all these briefs for Professor Tatum's class. I don't know how I'm going to get all this reading done in a single week."

"Let me guess." She slipped out of the chair and knelt down to help. "You're a first-year."

"Is it that obvious?"

"Yes," she said and smiled. "But it's not just you. I can spot a first-year a mile away."

She held out a hand. "Courtney Anderson."

Juliette froze, pretending to be surprised. "Oh my God. Your father is Governor Anderson. I saw you at the rally the other day. I didn't even recognize you."

Her smile grew even bigger. Note to self. Inflating the ego is a good thing.

"Are you interested in politics?" she asked.

"Oh, God no," Juliette said. "Living outside of D.C. for the last twelve years is about all the politics I can handle. You can't throw a stone without hitting some new politician."

She laughed. "Then why did you go to the rally?"

"I was just trying to earn a little extra credit. Hagney is a sucker for anyone involved in a political campaign. He said he's d give us five extra points for every rally we attended. All we have to do is write a paper reflecting on our experience. I swear, it's like high school all over again."

Juliette stacked the last of the briefs onto the pile and lifted them to the table. Courtney stood as well, but didn't bother to take her seat. Instead she glanced down at the paper on the top of the stack.

"The Keating Five?"

Juliette smiled. "Yeah. We're studying the legal aspects to some of the great political scandals of the twentieth century. Given the current state of our economy, I thought this would be an interesting one to study."

Now she had Courtney's attention.

"I wrote a brief on the mismanagement of the Keating Five investigation but Professor Tatum refused to publish it. She said it was politically motivated."

"Isn't everything?"

Courtney smiled. "You should come by the RNC later. I'm working on the Tyler Chase campaign. We could use some more bodies. Plus, I'll let you take a look at my notes on the Keating Five."

It was exactly what Juliette had hoped for. Though she would have preferred to avoid the Chase campaign altogether. "I don't know." She hesitated, not wanting to act too eager at the invitation. It was important to let Courtney believe working at the campaign was entirely her idea.

"Why not? If you tell Hagney you're an intern on the campaign, you can probably skip class completely. And everyone knows his class is pointless."

"Yeah, but I'm sure Senator Chase has other, more qualified people to work on his campaign."

"Nonsense. He's relying upon the college vote, which means college volunteers working on his campaign are invaluable. Plus he's the youngest U.S. Senator in office. The last person to get elected as a U.S. Senator this young went on to become Vice President of the United States. How can you pass up a chance like that?"

Courtney was right about one thing. Juliette couldn't pass up the opportunity to work for Tyler Chase, not if it meant she got an all access pass to Courtney Anderson.

Chapter 7:

The Campaign Stop

For the next two weeks Juliette did an impeccable job of avoiding Senator Chase at all costs. Which wasn't easy when she worked for the man's re-election campaign. Then Courtney called her late Saturday night after coming down with a horrendous case of food poisoning, and begged her to accompany Winston and Tyler on their media blitz across the state. Apparently she had lined up six live TV interviews with local anchors in key media markets. Their opponent, Robertson, had already confirmed his interview slots and there was no way the Senator could back out.

"I still don't understand how that makes me essential?" Juliette moaned. "I'm sure Tyler and Winston can manage just fine without me."

"No. Tyler gets anxious on camera. He needs someone to calm him down, keep him from getting all worked up."

"Isn't that what Winston is for?"

Courtney sighed. "Think of it as good cop, bad cop. Winston has to be the bad cop. He has to be brutally honest with Tyler to ensure he doesn't do or say anything that will screw up their messaging. I need you to be the good cop. Just cheer him on, lend an ear when he needs to rant about Winston or the biased reporter conducting the interview."

"I don't know." Juliette picked at her chipped fingernail polish. "I barely know him. How am I supposed to be the good cop?"

"He likes you! He's said as much to me before. I promise this will all work out. I'd go. If I could stand for five seconds without passing out."

Juliette gave in. But only because not doing so would put her on Courtney's bad side, and she couldn't afford that.

Now she was standing in the back of the darkened studio, marveling as Tyler Chase worked his magic. The first three interviews had gone spectacularly. The fourth not so much. The minute the three of them stepped out of the studio lot Tyler and Winston went at it. They barked at each other for ten minutes straight. Then Tyler insisted he needed space. He snatched the keys for the SUV out of Winston's hand and told him to go rent a car.

Juliette leaned against the car door unsure what she was supposed to do. Tyler stormed around the back of the vehicle and Winston jerked his head to the side. "Go with him," he muttered. Then he turned and walked back to the studio.

The whole thing was childish. Taking two separate cars seemed a lot of extra trouble just to please the senator. But when she climbed into the SUV she understood why Winston had been so willing to find his own way to the next lot. Tyler rambled on about the interview, cursing the reporter and spouting out inaccurate stats about his stance on gun control.

As if the gods could hear him, the sky opened up and a heavy downpour caused them to slow to a crawl. The only good thing was that Ty had stopped obsessing about his bad interview in order to focus on his driving. Thirty minutes later, when traffic came to a complete stop, his temper made a reappearance.

"We could get off at the next exit," Juliette suggested. "I can reroute the GPS and see if we can't find a way around the accident."

"Sure," he said as he inched toward the edge of the freeway. They drove along the berm of the road until they came to the next exit and then left the congested traffic behind them. That was Juliette's first mistake.

Chapter 8: Stuck

Juliette leaned back in the passenger seat and stared out the window as Tyler paced back and forth in the rain. He was desperately trying to get traction under the front tires, but so far was having absolutely no luck. Everywhere she looked there was mud. Sloppy, slimy, slippery mud. Unless Ty transformed into Superman and lifted the whole damn SUV into the air, they were stuck.

After a few long minutes Ty came to the same conclusion and climbed back into the car.

"It looks like we're stuck here."

Juliette rolled her eyes. As if she needed Mr. Obvious to relay that very important bit of information.

"What? It's not my fault the road is flooded." Ty jammed the keys into the ignition and started the car. He busied himself with the radio dials. Country. Commercial. Country. News. Country.

"Would you cut it out?" Juliette was close to her breaking point. "You're never going to find anything decent on the radio this far away from civilization."

Out of spite, Ty stopped on one of the country stations and turned up the volume.

A twangy song came on and he drummed his fingers against the steering wheel.

Juliette stared at him in amazement. "There is no way you like this song."

"Like it," he said, "I love it." And then he began singing the words in his best Keith Urban impersonation.

Juliette couldn't help laughing. The image of Tyler Chase, soaking wet in his two-thousand-dollar suit, singing car karaoke to a country song was more than she could bear. As the song reached its pivotal climax Ty shook his head like a shaggy wet dog and drops of water sloshed everywhere.

"Gross! You're getting me all wet."

She bent over to wipe her face with the bottom of her t-shirt. When she sat up again, Ty had ditched the jacket and was pulling a white t-shirt over his head, revealing that unmistakably perfect set of silky-smooth abs.

Juliette was no longer thinking about country music. She was barely thinking at all. It took every ounce of her concentration to keep from reaching out to him. All she could think about was the heat of his skin pressed against hers. And all she wanted to do was fuck him good and hard.

This realization brought Juliette back to her senses. "What are you doing?" She redirected her gaze to something, anything but Tyler Chase.

"I'm drying off." Ty rubbed the bunched-up t-shirt over his now bare chest. "I hate wet clothes."

"I thought you were like a world-class swimmer, or something."

"That's different. Speedos are meant for the water. Business attire is not."

Juliette had a flash of him in a Speedo. Those muscular glutes and tight ass, not to mention a sizable endowment that would strain against the seams of the fabric.

Juliette jerked and her knee banged against the console.

Ty gave her a curious glance. "You okay over there?"

She nodded.

"Because I hear the image of me without clothes can have quite an effect on the opposite sex."

Do not listen to him, she told herself. *Tyler Chase is off the market. Sleeping with him would be wrong.* Juliette hadn't known better the first time. That was on Tyler. But this time--no, there would be no this time.

"Seriously, are you okay?"

"Just put your clothes back on," Juliette muttered. "All we need is for someone to find us out here on the side of the road half-dressed."

"We aren't doing anything wrong."

"And I don't intend to," Juliette added. She jerked open the door and jumped out into the rain. There had to be a way to get out of this stupid situation.

She heard the sound of the car door slamming shut. Ty yelled something, but it was difficult to hear over the noise of the rain. Ty trucked around the front of the SUV and headed straight for her. He added his suit jacket to his ensemble, but his chest was still bare beneath it and his beautifully toned abs were still very visible. And wet.

Her body grew tense at the sight of him. She knew what he was going to say. That she was being ridiculous, that they should get back in the car before they both catch pneumonia.

Instead, Ty grabbed her by the shoulders and shoved her against the side of the door. She had only a moment to watch as those blue eyes drank her in, then he was kissing her, hard. His full lips pressed against hers, parting them quickly so that his tongue could explore deeper places. His hands slid up from her shoulders to her neck and then he buried his fingers in her hair. He moved closer, eliminating all distance between them, and she felt her nipples harden as his bare chest pressed against her. Her hips ground into him, wanting more, needing more. And then her hands dropped lower, cupping his tight ass, and he practically moaned in her mouth.

Suddenly his hands were pulling at her shirt and tracing the top line of her lace panties. He dipped lower to kiss her neck. Juliette gasped for fresh air. Without his lips on hers she began to think clearly. And by the time he undid the snap on her low-rise jeans she dug up enough of her ethics to shove him away.

Ty was not a small guy but he was distracted, and Juliette's shove caught him off guard. He slid backward in the mud and nearly fell to the ground.

"I'm sorry," Juliette said before he could question her. "We can's t. Courtney is my friend." Well, that was kind of a lie, but even if she was her enemy, it didn't change the fact that sleeping with another woman's man was wrong.

Dirty, maybe.

Hot, definitely.

But wrong.

So what? the dark side of her purred. *You think you're getting past those pearly gates? You're an aspiring con artist. Your parents were art thieves and your godparents fence stolen objects to the highest bidder. You've already got a first-class ticket to hell. Nothing you do with Ty is going to change that.*

Juliette turned away. She opened the passenger door but couldn't bring herself to get back into the vehicle. Instead, she grabbed her purse and slammed the door shut again. Then she headed for the mud-covered road.

"What are you doing?" Ty jogged after her.

"I'm going to get help. There's got to be a gas station or farm or something on this road. And who knows, maybe we'll get cell reception along the way."

"I'm not letting you go off on your own."

"I don't recall asking for your permission."

Juliette trudged along in the mud, her black and white Converse sneakers sliding along the gunk with each step. Ty reached out to steady her.

"I'm fine." Juliette pulled her arm away.

He dropped his arm and he walked silently beside her in the pouring rain.

Chapter 9:

The Dysfunctional Motel

Juliette and Tyler were beyond drenched by the time they reached the nearest town. If you could call it that. They came to a rundown motel that looked straight out of the seventies.

"Thank God," Juliette muttered under her breath. Her feet were killing her and her skin was ice-cold. A single bell chimed as Tyler held open the door and Juliette ran inside. The heat was like waking up in the tropics. She could just curl up on the floor and drink in the warmth.

A woman in her late sixties sat behind the counter fiddling with an all-weather radio that was mostly picking up static. She didn't look up until Tyler cleared his throat.

"Don't bother asking," she said. "We ain't got no power in half the rooms. The other half are already full."

"There aren't any cars in the lot," Ty said.

"I didn't see you show up in some fancy town car."

She had a point. Still, Juliette found it hard to believe that more than one couple had walked to this fine establishment.

Juliette strode over to the wall of brochures and newspapers. There was nothing interesting, a few pamphlets about camping and other outdoor stuff she didn't find appealing. She picked up a flyer on kayaking and laughed at the irony. Maybe if they were lucky a canoe would just float right past them and they could paddle their way back to civilization.

Juliette turned back to the counter, but not before loosening the screws on the leg of the table and nudging it a tad to the right. It leaned precariously forward. Then she stepped back to join Ty who was still trying to convince the woman that they would take any available room no matter what the condition.

"I'll pay you double the going rate."

She shook her head. "It's against company policy. I'm not losing my job for you two Yankees."

Juliette started to laugh but realized she was serious. She was so used to being in NYC that she sometimes forgot Virginia was south of the Mason-Dixon Line.

Just as the old woman smacked her palm on the back of the radio the rickety side table collapsed, sending pamphlets and knickknacks flying. Ty and the woman rushed toward the mess. Juliette, on the other hand, tossed the extra pamphlet behind the counter and disappeared on the other side. On her way up she swiped a random key from the board and slipped it into her jeans pocket.

"Damn table," the woman swore. "I hate this place. I tell you, something is always breaking. Always."

Juliette grabbed Ty by the elbow and pulled him toward the door. "We should go. It looks like you have your hands full and I'm certain if we get some gas and maybe a bag of sand or salt for traction, we can get our car moving again."

Ty looked at Juliette as if she had spoken a foreign language. He started to protest but caught the, "we need to get the hell out of here now," look in her eyes.

They pushed through the door, another set of chimes bid them well, and they were suddenly back in the rain.

"We walked two miles in the rain to get here. I'm not trudging back another two in this rain just so we can spend the night in a cramped SUV. Not when there's a perfectly dry bed right here."

"I agree," Juliette stepped into the darkness, where she was certain the hotel manager could not see her, and fished out the key from her pocket.

Ty stared at her hand as he processed this new development. A sly grin spread across his face. He pulled Juliette close and kissed her forehead. "Consider me impressed. Did you work that whole thing with the table and the brochures too?"

Juliette nodded. He kissed her again then took the key from her and squinted down at the number.

"I've never been so happy to spend the night in what might possibly be the world's shadiest hotel," Juliette said.

"This isn't so bad. Trust me, I've seen worse. And there's no indication that they charge by the hour."

They walked to the last door on the far side of the motel and stopped at room 12A. Ty stuck the key into the lock and pushed open the door. He hesitated before entering, as if he expected someone to jump out and yell, "Surprise!" But that didn't happen. He reached for the switch on the side the wall. It clicked on but there was still no light.

"She was right. No power."

Juliette pulled out her cell phone. She still didn't have a signal, but the phone was fully charged and the white glow of the screen gave them enough light that they could enter the room without running into furniture.

From what she could tell, there was a large dresser on the left side of the room with an ancient box TV set and a small ice bucket. To the right was the largest king bed she had ever seen. Though it might have just felt that way at the time, considering she really, really wanted to find two doubles.

In the back was a bathroom. The sink and mirror were in a little alcove that was open to the rest of the room. The shower and toilet at least had a door with a lock.

"So you're going to sleep on the floor, right?"

"Not a chance in hell," Ty said. "I'm pretty sure they don't vacuum the carpets in a place like this."

"Don't be such a snob," Juliette said. "I'm sure it's clean."

"I'm a Republican. I'm allowed to be a snob." He collapsed on the corner of the bed. "Yep. I'm good right here. Unless you want to sleep on the floor. By all means, be my guest."

"You're getting the bed wet," she scolded. "That's most definitely your side." Juliette stepped past him and headed for the bathroom. She was cold and wet and anxious to get out of the heavy clothes that clung to her skin. If they had been at a nicer hotel they might have had spare robes, but here they were lucky to get clean towels.

Juliette turned back to face Tyler. "Here's the thing," she said. "I need to know that you are going to be on your best behavior tonight."

Ty grinned. "Aren't I always?"

"I mean it. I'm cold and I'm tired and I'm pretty sure I am going to come down with some kind of pneumonia if I don't get out of these clothes."

He froze.

"So I'm taking a shower. And when I am done, I am going to dry off and sleep in one of these towels. Maybe while I'm doing that you can make some kind of pillow barricade to divide up the bed."

"What are we, fourteen?"

"I'm serious. Nothing is going to happen tonight."

Ty shrugged and watched her disappear into the bathroom.

Chapter 10:

Nighttime Rituals

Even in the dark the hot shower was like a little piece of heaven. Juliette let the warmth soak into her like liquid sunshine. If she could have, she would have stayed in the shower all night. At least then she would be warm. But that wasn't possible, nor was it fair. What if Ty wanted to take a shower and she used up what little hot water they had?

The thought of the senator naked was enough to make her jerk the faucet in the "off" direction. If she started lingering over images like that, this was going to be a very, very long night. Juliette traced her hand along for the shower curtain and pulled it aside so that she could climb out. Then she reached for the dingy towel and began to dry off.

Five minutes later she was standing with her hand on the doorknob. She checked the towel for the fifth time. It was knotted and secure. And there was no way in hell she was going to let it come off. Still, she couldn't make herself step out into the room where Ty was waiting. Maybe she should put on her old clothes again.

One look at the ice-cold and sopping wet jeans and she tossed that idea aside. She might as well go stand out in the rain again if she was going to do that.

Suck it up, Juliette.

She turned the knob and pulled the door open.

The silence in the room was almost as unnerving as the dark. For one horrifying moment she thought perhaps Tyler had left. Maybe he came to his senses and went to find another room.

But when she called out his name, his cell phone snapped on.

"Jesus. You scared me."

"Sorry." Ty sat up on the bed and then stood. "I was just enjoying the quiet." He moved toward her. Juliette fought the instinct to grab hold of her towel. "How was the shower?"

"The water's hot," she said. "For now."

He moved past her without a second glance and stepped into the bathroom.

Juliette hesitated, then, feeling a little stupid for not trusting Tyler to behave, she made her way to the bed.

The moment she sank into the lumpy mattress, all of the anxiousness and exhaustion piled up inside her. Once again she was alone with Tyler. Completely off the grid and putting everything she longed for at risk.

Juliette climbed under the blankets and tucked herself between the sheets. She chuckled softly as she bumped into the pillow barricade Ty had created. He had listened. Though some part of herself wondered if the fluffy border would be enough to keep them apart.

She closed her eyes and let herself drift off in the darkness.

She stirred when the mattress shifted beneath her. "Ty?" she called out. Though she wasn't certain why.

"Yeah?" he answered. Her heart fluttered at the sound of his voice.

She inched closer to the wall of pillows.

"What's wrong?"

She didn't answer him. She didn't have anything to say. Instead she reached her hand across the pillows, like a white flag. He scooted toward her and took her hand in his. Then they lay there like that. No speaking. Just being.

Chapter 11: Sweet Dreams

When Juliette awoke, her body was drenched in sweat and something heavy was draped across her waist. She glanced down. Ty's fingers rested near her belly button. She should have moved them, but there was something extremely comforting about their presence. And he was so peaceful resting beside her. His breathing--slow and heavy. In and out. Rise and fall.

A soft moonlight trickled in around the window shades. Juliette traced the back of Ty's hand. She dragged her fingers over his knuckles and up to his fingertips as she wondered what time it was and if the power had been restored.

She skimmed the rest of the room, searching for signs of electricity, but the alarm clock on the nightstand remained dark.

Looks like power is still one of the many things we don't have.

Juliette wriggled in the itchy bath towel.

Or clothes.

While she was sleeping, the knot at the front of her towel had come loose, but the material still hung loosely over her body. She was hesitant to secure it. After all, Ty was asleep and she was fully covered by the bed sheets. Though her pillow barricade had seen better days--one flattened pillow was trapped beneath Ty's body, the other had vanished.

She squiggled out of her towel and tossed it on the floor then let out a sigh of relief. The worn sheets were like silk against her skin.

Juliette imagined Ty lying beside her and wondered if he too was draped in a towel. Or perhaps he had simply slipped between the sheets with nothing on at all? His bare chest buried into the mattress and that perfectly round rear end caressing the sheets. His beautiful cock ready and free.

Her stomach clenched and she let out a gasp of surprise.

The air around her stilled. As if Ty was aware of her thoughts, he scooted closer, gripping her waist a little tighter, and she felt her heart skip a beat.

Wake him up. Wake him up now!

But she didn't.

And it would have been so easy. All she had to do was push him away. Roll him over and rebuild the wall of pillows. But she was drunk with power. Consumed by the rush of heat she got at the feel of him next to her, his warmth melting into hers. She barely resisted the urge to inch sideways and press herself more firmly against him. Though his body was more than tempting. She studied each inhale and watched his arm rise and fall with her own longing breaths.

Nothing good would come of this.

But her body disagreed. She closed her eyes and prayed for forgiveness just before pressing into the mattress and scooting an inch to the left.

She paused, searching for any sign that Tyler was aware of her movements. But he remained still, his breathing unchanged.

See there. It's not the end of the world. Lighting didn't strike you down.

The entire right side of her body was now nestled against his and Juliette was quite certain Tyler was going commando. She grinned in the darkness as Ty's body settled against hers. He showed no signs of being awake.

With the length of him pressed against the curve of her thigh, she longed for the hot, sweaty sex they shared only a month ago. They had been strangers then, which had only made it hotter. Being anonymous meant she could do whatever she wanted, say whatever she wanted. And she had.

The first time was fast: a sprint to the release. She had barely made it into the hotel room before Ty yanked her pencil skirt up to her waist and ripped off her white lace panties. She allowed his hands to explore her newly exposed skin and he groaned at the moistness already forming between her thighs. He kissed her deeply as he guided her farther into his suite. Though they never made it to the actual bedroom. Instead, they stumbled through the living room until they collided with a large mahogany desk. With a grunt of pure testosterone, Ty lifted Juliette up into the air and placed her on top of the desk. Then he dipped downward so that his mouth could replace his fingers.

Juliette fell back against the desk, arching and swaying against the chilled wood as Tyler buried himself between her legs. She found herself dizzy with every earth-shattering flick of his tongue.

Oh God. Juliette opened her eyes.

Her pulse was racing in her ears, making it difficult to assess Tyler's breathing. Was he still sleeping? What if he sensed the growing sexual tension inside her?

The memory of Ty's touch was enough to drive her crazy. She wanted to let her hand sink lower, but it was impossible with his arm still draped across her waist. *He's asleep. He wouldn't notice anything if you don't squirm around too much.*

No. It was tempting but completely inappropriate. She could not feel herself up with Ty lying right beside her. Out of the question.

But the idea nagged at her. Her body practically purred at the memory of him. This was the next best thing to having him.

She traced another finger over his arm and waited to see if he showed any sign of life. When she was convinced that Ty wouldn't wake, she dropped her hand lower and let herself drift back into the glorious memory of him.

It was next to impossible to constrain herself. Her hips wanted to thrust forward. Her back wanted to arch backward. She wanted masculine hands to explore her body and Ty's succulent lips to kiss her skin.

She froze and took in a sharp breath in an effort to control herself, then realized to her horror that the steady breathing beside her had stopped. Instead, there were raspy, short breaths coming much too fast for her liking.

She didn't have to open her eyes to know Tyler was awake. She felt the length of his hardness pressing against her thigh.

Her leg twitched at the movement and both of them moaned in pleasure. The floodgates had opened and her resistance had completely shattered. She thrust her own hips upward, massaging herself with her fingers. Ty let out another groan and tightened his grip on her waist. He rolled her onto her side and inched forward so that he melted into the backside of her body. Then he dropped his hand lower, covering her small fingers with his own. Juliette gave him control, following his lead as he guided her own hand over the smooth skin between her legs and wound her like a tightened coil. His cock pressed into her from behind and she found herself oddly turned on by the sensation. She rubbed up against him, grinding and twisting, her moans filling the darkened room. He groaned loudly and inched her body toward the headboard.

"I want to fuck you now," he said.

All Juliette could do was nod.

Ty traced his hand down the length of her leg and lifted it up at the knee. Then he expertly slipped inside her. She exhaled deeply. The shock of his size made her body quiver and she cried out as he pulled himself back out.

"You like that," Ty said.

Juliette nodded again.

"You want more?"

She answered him with her hips, dipping lower to meet him. He plunged inside her a second time. This time he stayed inside her, grinding against her ass one delicious inch at a time. Up and down, in and out, he was teasing her and she didn't know how long she could take it.

His hand traced the length of her inner thigh and he began to stroke her from the front, overwhelming her in a way that no vibrator ever could. She found herself thrusting down to welcome each of Ty's jerks inside her. Juliette raised her hands to her chest, grabbing both of her breasts and rubbing her fingers over her nipples.

Ty gained speed. His hands clutched her waist, steadying her so that he could slam inside of her with more force. She welcomed each thrust with a deeper moan. It was so much better than she remembered. He gave a final thrust and burst inside her. His wetness was enough to send her over the edge and she felt the dam inside her break. She cried out again in dizzying pleasure just as Ty bent into her. They froze as one, riding the wave of pleasure. After a few seconds Ty raised his head and began kissing her neck. He didn't bother to pull out of her and Juliette was glad. She wanted to claim that magic penis as her own. As long as it was buried inside her, he was hers. But they couldn't stay like that forever, and Juliette was sorry to say, she wasn't the first one to pull away.

Chapter 12: Regrets

"I'm going to break up with her."

The *her* in that sentence would be Courtney. Well, at least he had the decency to not use her name. Still, the reminder of his current girlfriend doused any lingering fire between them. She didn't want to think about Courtney because if she did, she would only be reminded of how much she had screwed everything up. No Courtney, no Dean. No chance at the truth about her parents' murder.

Her animal instincts told her to screw Courtney. But that wasn't a realistic option. She at least needed to hold out until she saw this thing through with Dean.

"That's a nice offer, but you know you can't do that."

"I can do anything I want."

"No you can's t. You gave up that right the moment Governor Anderson appointed you as senator of Virginia. Now you're running for re-election-- something you didn't have to do to get the job in the first place, I might add. You think breaking up with his daughter is the best political move?"

Ty was silent as he processed her words.

She reached out for him, desperate to see his face.

"I don't love her. She's not you."

"You don't even know me," Juliette said.

He grinned and brushed the side of her arm. "After what we just did, I think I know you pretty well."

"I'm serious, Ty. You have an amazing political future ahead of you. Like it or not, Courtney is part of that future. She fits into this world in a way that I never will. Hell, she's practically Republican royalty."

His hand froze and he was quiet for a moment.

What was he thinking? That she was right? That he was too good for her?

Juliette continued speaking before she talked herself out of it. "I'm not going to tell her about us. So your secret is safe with me."

"What if I don't want it to be a secret?"

She grabbed his hand and lifted it from her shoulder. "You're a U.S. senator. You have to play by their rules or they'll chop off your head."

"They?"

"Take your pick. The Governor. The President. The RNC. The Media. The American people"

Ty was quiet again. She wanted desperately to know what he was thinking. The fact that he was putting up a fight made her feel victorious. She was his first choice. But Juliette couldn't indulge in those feelings. Ty only knew her as Jules, the Art History major and campaign volunteer. He didn't even know her real name, much less the fact that she was currently caught up in her own web of lies.

"This Isn't going to happen again," Juliette said. "You should get some rest. We have an early day tomorrow if we are going to get back to D.C. in time for the morning news cycle."

Chapter 13: Making Peace

The morning was awkward. Juliette woke up early so that she could shower and change and then headed down to the front desk to see if she could swipe some candy from the vending machines when the office clerk wasn't looking. Luckily the grouchy woman from the night before was not working the front desk. Instead there was an older gentleman with blotchy skin and graying hair. He wore a faded striped cardigan that looked as if it had been swiped straight from the Cosby Show. A pair of silver reading glasses was perched on his nose.

Just her luck. Juliette smiled at the sight of the man. She might be able to get some sympathy this time around.

The chime clanged as she pulled open the door and stepped inside. He looked up from his crossword and Juliette gave a hesitant smile before surveying the small room as if this were her first time seeing it.

"Can I help you?" he asked.

Juliette bit her lip and pondered the question before answering. "I'm not sure," she said finally. "I've been trying to get a signal here, for my cell phone, but I'm not having any luck."

He nodded. "I'm afraid the coverage is spotty around these parts. Of course I don't trust the damn things anyway. They give you cancer, you know"

Right. Cancer.

"You wouldn't happen to have a landline I could borrow? My car got stuck about a mile back. The roads out there are horrible. All that flooding. Does it flood like that a lot?"

He set the newspaper down and turned to face her in full. "We do get a lot of rain, but not like this. That sure was something, though. Those skies just opened up and wham, Noah's Ark might not have survived that one."

Juliette nodded in agreement. "I know. I wouldn't have come out in this weather at all, except my mother's vacationing with me and she forgot her medicine. We've been trying to get to the pharmacy so that we can refill the prescription."

The man's face collapsed with concern. "I hope she's okay. I've got the diabetes, and it's no fun."

Juliette nodded. She had spotted the medical alert tag on his wrist. That, combined with the open bag of sugar-free jelly beans seated behind him, tipped her off.

"If I could just use your phone real quick, I think I might be able to call my friend to come and help us?"

"There are phones in the rooms," the man said, suddenly remembering his job.

I gave myself a mental snap in the head.

Of course there were phones in the rooms. But her room was one without power. She had just assumed that with no power the phones would be down as well. Clearly that was not the case.

Think fast, Juliette. You need a good reason to explain why you are such a moron. When in trouble, go back to the truth. It's less difficult to screw up.

"Oh I'm sorry. I didn't stay here. I just was passing by and this was the first shelter I came to. I figured you might be used to weary travelers in need of assistance." She tilted her head slightly and gave the most pleading look she could with her brown eyes.

His eyes met hers for a few seconds. She wasn't certain if he was searching for truth or the courage to tell her no. So she played her trump card.

"I'm sorry. Never mind. This was too much of an imposition. I'll keep searching for a signal."

He jumped from the chair and moved around the counter.

"No. No," he said. "A young girl like you shouldn't be wandering around alone." He grabbed the heavy rotary phone and placed it on the counter in front of her.

"Wow. I haven't seen one of these in" She thought about it. "Ever?"

"I'd expect not. Do you know how to use it?"

"I don't have a college degree in engineering, but I think I can figure it out," she paused. "You know what would be helpful though? A fresh cup of coffee."

She nodded to the mug on the counter and gave her best smile. The old man hesitated at first but then gave in. "I think that can be arranged." He trudged off into the back room.

Juliette waited until she was certain he was out of earshot and then pulled a piece of paper out of her pocket. She dialed the number, already nervous about what she was going to say. She didn't want to call Courtney, but she didn't have Winston's number in her phone. She could have waited for Ty, but the less she had to interact with him the better.

"Hello," Courtney's high voice rang through the receiver.

"Hey, Courtney. Are you busy?"

"Jules? What's up? How's the media blitz going?"

"Not so well it seems. We got lost during some pretty bad storms yesterday and now we're stranded outside of Buckingham or Cumberland. I'm not sure which."

"Oh my God, that's awful."

"I was just hoping maybe you could send someone from the local field office out to meet me."

"I guess."

Juliette could hear the suspicion in her voice.

"Look, I know Tyler's your boyfriend, but he's kind of intimidating, you know. I'm nervous enough as it is. I don't want to look like a complete idiot in front of him."

This time she gave a slight laugh. "Yeah. I get what you mean. There's definitely an intensity about Tyler Chase."

Honey, you have no idea.

"I'll call Melissa. She's working in the Richmond office today. She will come get you, no questions asked. Just give me the address and I'll send her a text."

"There's no cell service here. Well, at least not with my carrier."

She paused. "Hang tight. I'll see what I can do and call you back at this number in ten minutes."

They said goodbye and Juliette glanced up at the hotel manager who was back to doing his crossword. A not so fresh mug of luke-warm coffee sat on the counter.

"She's going to find someone to pick me up," Juliette said. "Then we can hopefully get my car unstuck."

He nodded but was too caught up in his puzzle to pay her any real attention. She wandered over to the vending machine to check out the goods. It was your typical salty and sweet fare. Only it didn't exactly look as if it got refreshed that often. There was a bag of chips on the third row that still had the Super Bowl logo on the corner. Win tickets, it said. Hmm. Pretty sure that game had come and gone nine months ago. On second thought, maybe she's d better pass on the food.

The door chimed and Tyler walked in. Thank God he was fully clothed.

Chapter 14: A Cry for Help

In the glass of the vending machine Juliette could see Tyler staring at her. Confused.

"Jules," he said, and she fought the urge to turn around. He was going to ruin everything.

"Hey," he moved farther into the lobby.

"I'm sorry," she turned around and his face relaxed. "Do I know you?"

The frown lines returned. "Huh?"

"You look familiar, but I can't place it." Juliette turned to her new friend behind the counter. "Doesn't he look familiar?"

The old man studied Tyler closely before nodding in agreement. "Yeah. He sure does. What do you do, son? You someone famous or something?"

Or something was right.

"Not famous, just a politician."

"That's right. The great senator. Replaced that guy Reis, God rest his soul. He was a good man."

At that neither Ty nor Juliette knew what to say. So they stood in silence. Ty searching desperately for some clue of what was going on and Juliette trying to remain distant. It was harder than she would have guessed.

"So, what's your platform?" she said. Continuing with the charade that she had never met him before. A little improv storytelling was always good practice.

Ty took the bait.

"Well, I'd like to think I'm continuing the legacy that Senator Reis left. We share a lot of the same views on family values and hard work."

The old man nodded. "Hard work. That's one thing I have to wonder if any of you young folks know something about. It seems everyone wants to take the easy way out. Like having a Senate seat handed to them on a gold platter by the governor of Virginia instead of paying your dues."

Uh-oh. This wasn't going to go well.

"I take it your a Robertson supporter?"

He grunted. "Nope. I only throw my support behind men who actually stand for something. You politicians nowadays, you dress up in spiffy suits and act like you're king of the world but you don't do squat to make a difference. I'm not willing to hand over my vote to just any who-ha that smiles my way."

Tyler chewed on this for a moment but he didn't seem particularly unraveled.

"Tell me more." He stepped closer to the counter and leaned down as if to get settled in for a long conversation.

Just then the phone rang.

"Dillwyn Motel," he said before handing Juliette the phone.

She grabbed the receiver and backed away from the two men. Thankfully the hotel manager seemed eager to continue their conversation and they paid Juliette little attention.

"Okay. So here's the plan," Courtney started and she began to relay the details of Juliette's rescue. She jotted everything down on the back of a pamphlet. She noticed the table hadn't been put back together and felt little guilty about it. She made a mental note to slip them a twenty before leaving. They did after all provide room and board, even if they didn't know it.

Juliette hung up the phone and headed for the door.

"You got everything all figured out?" the old man called after her.

"Yes, thanks. Someone is on the way. I'm just going to stand outside so that they can see me."

Juliette made her way to the door without a second glance at Ty or the old man. She didn't want either of them to convince her to stay. In fact, part of her was hoping that the hotel manager would keep Ty occupied in deep conversation until her ride appeared. It sounded as if they were only fifteen minutes away by car, maybe less.

But then she heard those damn chimes and turned around to see Ty following her.

"What?" she snapped before he could say anything.

"Did I do something wrong?" he asked. "Because you seem to be avoiding me today."

Juliette stared at him. *Did he do something wrong? Of course he did. They both did.* "I don't want to talk to you, Ty. I thought I made that clear last night."

"First you tell me to behave, keep my distance. Then I wake up and you're practically dry humping my leg."

Juliette's face burned red and she swatted him on the arm. "Will you not say that so loud? People can hear you."

"Hey, I'm not complaining. To tell you the truth, I rather enjoyed it."

"Of course you did. But there's not going to be a repeat performance. I had a serious lapse of judgment. And now I am going to do everything I can to make sure that doesn't happen again."

"Oh come on Jules. Don't do this. I told you I would break up with Courtney. It's not going to short-circuit my campaign. I like you. What more do you want from me?"

"I don't want anything from you!" Juliette cried and then realized how loud she was yelling. She needed to get away from him, not just because they were starting to cause a scene, but because he was talking her into something she knew she shouldn't do.

"Jules." He jogged after her and she batted him away. She would walk all the way to the car if she had to. She just couldn't stand to be near him. But he grabbed her shoulders and forced her to stop. When he turned her around his face shifted from anger to sadness. "Are you crying?"

"No." But that was a lie. Her cheeks were wet and she hadn't even noticed. She wiped one trail of tears away with the back of her hand. "It's nothing. I'm fine."

He ignored her completely and pulled her into his arms. This time she didn't fight him. She just rested her head against his chest and tried to tell herself that everything would be all right. But at that moment she wasn't so sure. Because in Ty's arms she felt safe and she felt loved and nothing else seemed to matter at that precise moment, on the edge of the parking lot of the Dillwyn Motel.

"We can't do this." She pulled away from him.

He opened his mouth to speak, but she held up a finger to his lips.

"Don't say it. I don't want to live with the memory of you professing what I think you want to profess. I know you don't get it, but if you really do care about me, you will give me some space. Just let me go, for now. Please let me go."

At that moment a car horn honked and they both jumped backward. *They weren't doing anything, right? So why did they look so damn guilty?*

"Is that Melissa?" Ty asked.

Juliette smiled. "She's our ride." The spunky girl with the pixie cut rolled down the passenger side window. "What the hell happened to you guys?"

"Trust me," Ty said. "You don't want to know."

Only, as Juliette climbed into the backseat, Melissa gave her peculiar look. It seemed to her that Melissa wanted to know very, very badly.

Chapter 15: News Break

Back in her Georgetown apartment Juliette was able to reassure herself that she had done the right thing, despite the fact that Tyler appeared to be following the plan. The day after their disastrous trip through Virginia, Courtney cornered her in the lobby of the GWU student union. Juliette had been certain she was in for a beat down. But Courtney gave her a big hug, took her by the hand, and dragged her into the Java Joint.

They spent an hour talking about the campaign and other than a comment about how happy she was that Juliette was safe, Courtney made not one comment about her being stranded in the hills of Virginia.

Now, a week later, she was sitting at Courtney's apartment, watching CNN and stuffing envelopes for a mailer due to go out over the next two days.

"Do you want iced tea or lemonade?" Courtney called from the kitchen, where she was making popcorn and fixing drinks.

"Tea."

Courtney glided across the floor, balancing two glasses of ice in one hand and a pitcher of iced tea in the other. She set each one down on a coaster. Her eyes widened as she glanced up at the muted television set.

"Hey, are they talking about Tyler?"

They were talking about him, or at least that's what it looked like with the sound off. Courtney reached for the remote and clicked the volume on. But all they managed to catch was, "We will have more on this story and what CNN learned about Senator Chase and his new mystery woman in a moment."

Courtney sank down slowly into the couch like a deflated toy. "What did she just say?"

Juliette couldn't speak. Even if she could find her voice, what would she say? It was insulting to deny the truth, especially if the news outlets were already broadcasting details of their relationship. It was probably all over every Twitter and Facebook account in America, certainly D.C.

This can't be happening. We were careful. We broke it off.

But they weren't careful. Not really. Any yahoo with a phone could have overheard their conversations or snapped a picture of the two of them together. In the car, at the TV studios. Or the motel

"It's probably nothing to worry about," Juliette managed. But she was far from convincing.

A flashy musical beat accompanied Tyler's picture on the TV screen. The blonde anchor was practically grinning as she reported the breaking news.

"CNN recently learned from an exclusive source that Senator Tyler Chase is not the faithful man he claims to be. The senator was caught embracing an unknown woman in the parking lot of the Dillwyn Motel. Our sources say Chase was passing through the small town of Dillwyn on a media tour to major news networks throughout the state of Virginia. This morning the following photo was sent to CNN from an anonymous source."

A photo appeared in the middle of the screen. Juliette held her breath as she stared at her and Ty in the parking lot. It had to have been taken by Melissa. No one else knew where they were. She had hoped Courtney's friend hadn't spotted them together. But clearly she was wrong.

She waited for Courtney to say something but there was only silence. When she looked over at Courtney the expression on her face said it all. She was pissed. Beyond pissed.

"It's not what you think," Juliette said. Her instinct was simply to keep Courtney from strangling her. "That photo was taken out of context."

"That's you and Tyler, right?"

"Yes, but please believe me. Nothing happened." Juliette didn't know why she said it. It was just that every instinct in her was telling her to lie. Deny, deny, deny.

"You didn't say Senator Chase was at the motel with you."

Uh-oh. She was using Tyler's full title. That was a bad sign. And what did she say? The truth was awful.

"Yes. Tyler was there. But it is not what you think."

"Then tell me what I should think, because that picture raises a shit load of questions."

Juliette couldn't meet her eyes. They were fiery and dangerous as if they could rip her apart with one cold glare. She was prepared for this. She practiced the story a million times in her head. But now she struggled to get the words out. She wasn't stupid enough to believe that the conversation would never come up, but she hadn't expected a photo to make its way into the evidence piled against her.

"I have diabetes," Juliette spat out. Please, God, let this work.

"What does that have to do with anything?" Courtney's eyes scanned Juliette up and down, as if looking for a diabetes label branded on her skin.

"I've had it since I was a little girl. I take insulin shots twice a day."

"I've never seen you take a shot."

"That's because I prefer to keep it quiet. People get uncomfortable when you pull out a needle and shoot up in front of them, even if it is for a completely legitimate reason."

Juliette raised the corner of her shirt to reveal the tiny scar marks on her stomach. The marks were real, but they weren't from insulin. Juliette used a sterile needle, saline solution, and makeup to create the effect of old marks on her skin. At the time she had been convinced she was just being overly paranoid. But now she was grateful she took the extra steps. The needle marks sold the idea of Juliette as a diabetic.

"So what does your diabetes have to do with the photo?"

"We got lost during the storm. The SUV was stuck in the mud and we abandoned the vehicle near the flooded-out road. It was a stupid mistake. Carrying insulin with you at all times is like the first thing they teach you when you're diagnosed. But I left it in the cubby on the side of the passenger door."

Courtney's face softened, but only slightly.

"Tyler and I hiked to the motel, but it took hours. And with no food my blood sugar dropped. I got sick and was incredibly embarrassed. Ty was amazing. He got me a room and some hot food. He stayed by my side to make sure I was okay. He's such a good guy, Courtney. He even promised to keep my secret.

"That picture was taken right before Melissa picked us up. I was tired and grateful for all that he had done. It was a completely platonic hug, nothing more. A thank-you."

There was a light buzzing sound from the coffee table. Courtney slid over to glance at her phone. "It's not me." She eyed Juliette's bag. Juliette pulled the phone out of the side pocket and stared at the screen.

Tyler Chase. She probably should have deleted his number. That would have been a smart move.

"I don't have to answer it."

Courtney folded her arms over her chest. "Yes you do. Clearly he wants to talk to you more than he does me."

The phone buzzed again and Juliette was tempted to hit decline.

But Courtney's voice lashed out at her. "Answer it," she demanded. "Now."

Juliette swiped the screen and raised the phone to her ear.

Chapter 16: Spin City

The voice that greeted Juliette was filled with worry. "I just got a zillion text messages about a photo that's leaked to the press."

"Yeah, I know. I'm staring at it now." Juliette locked eyes with Courtney.

"I'm so sorry. I don't know how that got out there."

"Yeah, well it Isn't your fault. You were just trying to be nice. The snitch who took the photo didn't know that."

He hesitated and Juliette struggled to fill the silence. She needed to clue him in without tipping off Courtney that this whole story was just an act.

"Don't worry, I already explained everything to Courtney."

"You've talked with Courtney?" His voice was steady.

"I'm sitting right beside her actually. We're stuffing campaign mailers."

"Wait. What?"

"Senator Chase, don't apologize. I know I asked you to keep all this between us. I didn't want people treating me differently because of my diabetes. But Courtney deserved to know the truth."

"So she knows?" Tyler asked.

"About the diabetes, yes. And though she's a bit upset about not knowing you stayed with me at the motel, I think she understands. Maybe you should talk to her though"

"Yeah. Can you put her on?"

She handed the phone to Courtney, who took it reluctantly.

Then Juliette grabbed her glass of iced tea and headed for the kitchen. She wanted to at least give Tyler and Courtney the illusion of privacy, even if she couldn't afford to be clueless about their conversation. She needed to be certain Courtney bought the story. She needed to keep the mark's trust. So she stood beside the island, drinking tea and merely pretending she was invisible.

Their conversation was brief and Courtney didn't give anything away. After a few nods and uh-huhs, she hung up and turned to Juliette.

"Tyler is on his way over."

What? That was not what she wanted. She needed to stay as far away from the senator as possible. It was hard enough keeping this charade up without his presence.

"I think I should go."

Courtney gave a half protest but it wasn't enough to be authentic. So she gathered her belongings and headed for the door.

Juliette was down in the first floor lobby when she spotted him. Tyler ran up to her, blocking her path. "You're leaving?"

"Of course I'm leaving. Your girlfriend is about two heartbeats away from discovering what a lying, cheating man-whore you are."

"Don't you think we should talk?"

"No. I'm done talking. Talking is what gets us in trouble."

"That's not true," he said. "Fucking is what gets us in trouble."

Juliette flailed her arms at him. "Say that a little louder. I don't think the entire first floor heard you."

Tyler took hold of her coat and steered her to the alcove past the elevator bay.

"We need to talk."

"No we don't. I already explained to Courtney what happened."

"And you don't think you should explain that to me as well, since I apparently was there?"

Juliette gave in. "What do you want to know?"

"Tell me everything you told Courtney."

She shrugged. "I already did. I told her that I have diabetes. That my sugar dropped and I got sick without my insulin. That you deposited me at the motel, scrounged up some food, and insisted I rest. I told her that I made you swear to keep my secret and that the photo was nothing more than me thanking you for being an absolute gentleman."

"But you don't have diabetes. What if she checks?"

Juliette raised the side of her shirt a second time. "I was diagnosed as a child. The scars are from years of injections.

Ty reached out to touch her stomach but she flinched at the movement. His hand froze in midair. "Those weren't there the other day."

"Are you sure? It's not like we had the lights on."

He frowned. "I'm sure. I have a photographic memory. Which means I have a very clear picture of what your body looks like naked and those were not there."

"So I embellished a little. Be grateful. These scars sell the story. It's not the greatest explanation, sure. It can't help with the smear on your political career, but it gives you some room to work things out with Courtney."

"How many times do I have to tell you I don't want to work things out?"

Juliette winced at the horrifying thought of Ty confessing everything to Courtney. What if he broke up with her? Juliette would never be able to regain her trust.

Juliette punched him hard in the shoulder.

"Oww. What the hell?" He pulled away from her. His eyes were flaming with anger.

She raised a hand again but didn't strike.

"You listen to me, Tyler Chase. You are going to go upstairs and apologize to your girlfriend. Do whatever you have to do to make it up to her. I've given you an in, but you have to pull the trigger." Juliette stepped closer. "I don't want to hear any more nonsense about breaking up with her. Because even if you do, this thing between us," she pointed at Ty and then herself, "it is never going to happen."

"Whatever it takes?"

"Whatever it takes."

Chapter 17:

The Mystery Date

Twenty-four hours passed without hide nor hair from Courtney and Ty. Juliette was on edge. Ty hadn't called her, which she had explicitly demanded he do in order to update her on what had happened.

Then this afternoon her cell phone pinged. It was a text from Courtney.

Sorry about yesterday. Hope to see you at the fundraiser tonight. Black tie only!

Yikes. In the mess of everything she had forgotten about the black and white charity ball at the Kennedy Center. And she didn't even have a dress. She had meant to get one the day before but with all the commotion the shopping had quietly fallen off her list. Now she stared at the text message wondering if Courtney was serious. Was this a sign that Courtney and Ty had made up? Had she really bought the story about the low blood sugar?

Juliette paced the living room, back and forth, at least ten times before tossing the phone on the couch where she could no longer see it. She didn't have time to question Courtney's intentions. Her job was to make nice with the girl and right now she was failing miserably. Juliette would take any white flag peace offering she could get, in hopes that she could get this job back on track.

There was a knock at the door. Juliette set the phone on the counter. She wasn't expecting company. Hell, it was one o'clock in the afternoon and she hadn't even showered and dressed yet. She ran a hand through her chestnut hair in a desperate attempt to smooth down the tangles.

This time she checked the peephole before opening the door. Only no one was there. At least not that she could see.

Maybe it was a prank? Or it could have been someone at her neighbor's door. Though she hadn't heard anyone greet any guests and welcome them in.

Juliette lifted the chain lock and cracked open the door so that she could take a peek. Yep. The hall was definitely deserted. She started to close the door again when she spotted a black and white box on her doorstep with a lavish silver bow.

Juliette knelt down and picked up the box. There was no card or note to tell her who it was from. The box itself was light, and when she shook it she could hear the soft rustle of the contents inside.

Juliette stepped back into her apartment, closing and locking the door behind her. She headed over to her dining room table. Carefully she untied the ribbon, split open the tape holding the lid in place, and lifted the top up to reveal a swath of red and white tissue paper. Beneath the first layer of paper was a shimmering black fabric.

She lifted the thin straps of a gown, revealing the most stunningly simple and yet gorgeous couture dress she had ever seen. The fabric was thin and smooth with a metallic sheen that would cling nicely to the curves of her body. The bodice had a plunging neckline that dipped to a few inches above the waist and was secured with a large antique diamond brooch. The item of jewelry alone was worth more than fifty thousand dollars.

Juliette turned back to the box and searched for a card. This gift was too much. She's d have to return it immediately. But who could have sent it? Only a handful of people knew she was planning on attending the charity ball. She had been added as a last-minute guest of Courtney Anderson.

Juliette spotted something red stuck between the folds of tissue paper. She reached for the envelope, ripped it open and skimmed the simple white note card inside.

"Thought you might find this useful."

There was no signature. That was not good. The only person who might send her such an extravagant gift and leave the card unsigned would be Tyler Chase.

That's it. You are so not going anywhere tonight.

Juliette dropped the dress back into the box and plodded over to the sofa. *Just watch some trashy TV show and blow off the whole damn thing.*

That proved to be easier said than done. Every commercial break, Juliette found her eyes drifting back to the white box. She found herself imagining the dress and what it might feel like to get all glammed up.

It won't hurt to try it on. It doesn't mean you have to attend.

No. She shoved the thoughts into the far corners of her mind.

A full episode of Grey's Anatomy passed before she finally gave in. If Meredith Grey could have her McDreamy, she could damn well try on a dress from a mystery stranger. *Maybe it wasn't from Tyler Chase at all.*

Yeah right. She couldn't even think that with a straight face.

Juliette grabbed the box and dashed into her bedroom before she gave herself time to abandon the idea. She stripped down to her panties and then undid the thin clasp. The gown was too thin and delicate to step into, especially with her curvy hips. So she carefully lifted it over her head and let it slink down around her body. She tugged gently until it lay crease-free against her like a second skin. When she turned to the full-length mirror on the back of her closet door her jaw dropped. Even barefoot and makeup free, with a tangle of unwashed hair, she looked amazing. The dark color brought out the richness of her skin. The deep v-cut showed off a mind-blowing amount of cleavage, and yet it was still tactful. And the diamond brooch, well, it sparkled and shined like it was the bow holding the entire dress together. She looked like a mouthwatering Christmas present, waiting to be unwrapped. And she loved it.

You can't go to that ball. Only bad things will come of it.

Juliette cast aside the warning. She was nearly giddy at the thought of walking into the ballroom at the Kennedy Center for the Arts in this dress. It had nothing to do with seeing Tyler Chase's reaction, she told herself. She just wanted to be seen. It was like the prom night she never had.

Juliette forced herself out of the dress and then began the frantic ritual of washing, waxing, and plucking to ensure her body was just as perfect as the dress she was donning. She sat at the vanity in her silk dressing gown and set her hair in hot curlers while singing along to the radio. While she waited for the curls to set she polished her nails, both fingers and toes, and then moved to her face. She did a deep smoky eye with silvers and grays that would accentuate the dark dress and a bold red lipstick. It was covered with a pale, shimmery powder that left her skin sparkling. An hour later she pulled out the curlers to reveal springy brown ringlets. She pulled the length of her hair into a loose knot and allowed the shorter curls to fall free around her face. And suddenly, she was ready for the Dress.

This time when she slipped into the gown she felt like royalty. Her body had been completely transformed and she was speechless at the finished product. She stared at her reflection in the mirror, barely recognizing herself in the person looking back at her. She looked like someone who donned the red carpet three times a week. Sure, she had spent hours to get the effect, but it was most definitely worth it.

Juliette stepped into a pair of simple black stiletto heels and grabbed a small clutch from the closet. She debated for a moment about taking a coat and after checking the weather decided to not take one would be foolish. It would be well after one when she made her way home and the temperatures would likely be in the forties. She was certain there would be a coat check anyway.

She grabbed her roommate's black wool coat with the gray faux fur collar and headed out the door. To her surprise a single yellow cab was pulling up in front of her building and a middle-aged couple climbed out. The man, spotting her elegant dress, held the door open for her as she climbed in. She thanked him and then gave the driver her directions.

To the Kennedy Center be damned.

Chapter 18: Pop Quiz

By the time her cab got through the bevy of cars waiting to drop off their passengers, the Kennedy Center was swarming with D.C.'s elite. Juliette had to pinch herself before climbing out of the taxi. This was the real deal. U.S. senators, congressional lobbyists, the defense secretary; just thinking about the guest list made her dizzy.

She had to remind herself that she wasn't here to network. Her target was still Courtney. The senator's daughter was the only person she needed to impress tonight.

At the steps of the entrance she hesitated. *What if someone recognizes you from the picture on the news? What if your presence raises even more suspicions?*

But that was silly. The photo only showed her from behind; no one had seen her face. Melissa, thank God, hadn't bothered to release a name with the papers, at least not yet. So there was no way anyone except for Courtney could even know it was her. And if Courtney was okay with her being here, that's all that mattered.

"Can I help you?" a voice asked her.

Juliette turned and saw Dean Covington smiling back her. He raised a hand before she could ask him any questions. "I'm here on official Covington and Crawford business. The governor is a very important client."

He took Juliette's left arm and escorted her inside. "I trust your new job is going well?"

Juliette nodded.

"Good. I was starting to worry you might not show tonight."

Her face flushed red. Did Covington suspect she was the mystery girl in the photo?

"Don't be embarrassed, darling. I hear Senator Chase can be quite charming when he wants to be. Just stick to the assignment and you'll be fine." He spun Juliette around to face the coat check before whisking her out of the heavy wool coat and handing over his own jacket along with a twenty-dollar bill. He informed the attendant to keep the change then placed the small white ticket in his tux pocket.

"Now go," he said. "Go grace the room with you stunningly beautiful presence."

Juliette gave a cautious smile and stepped toward the entrance of the hall. She hesitated, turned back to Covington, then realized he had vanished. The man had impeccable timing, she would give him that.

Juliette trudged up the glittering stairs and entered the ballroom. She was breathless. The space had been transformed into a magical silver and white wonderland. There wasn't a corner of the room that had been left untouched--from the large trees with twinkling white lights and silver globes hanging from the willowy branches to the mirrored tabletops and black-and-white skirted chairs gathered at each table. The dance floor was in the dead center of the room and had a series of sequined balls that sent lights twinkling and twirling over the crowd. A small orchestra was playing on a makeshift stage at the end of the room. Everywhere she turned there were servers with trays of champagne and hors d'oeuvres. She resisted the urge to take a glass.

She spotted Governor Anderson in a crowd of businessmen and politicians, but not his daughter. Then, as she was making her way to the cash bar, she spotted him. Senator Tyler Chase was standing on the other side of the dance floor. Staring at her and her stunning black dress. Juliette wanted to turn away, to run and hide from that unmasked look in his eyes. But she was paralyzed by his gaze. And as he moved closer to her, she realized with regret that she wanted him.

"You look amazing," he said.

"It's mostly the dress."

"No," he argued. "It's not."

His gaze moved from her shimmering shoulders to the round curve of her breasts to the large diamond brooch centered at her waist.

He started to reach for it but froze as if only then realizing what he was about to do.

"It's great Isn't it?"

"Yeah," he muttered.

Juliette couldn't make out the expression on his face. She thought he had sent the dress, but he was staring at the brooch as if in shock. As if he hadn't expected her to show up wearing it.

"It looks like an antique. Maybe something from the 1920's s. What do you think?" She tested her theory further.

Ty shook his head. "It looks familiar," he muttered. "But honestly, I have no idea."

He was lying, she could tell. His eyes were drawn to the jewelry as if it was calling out to him.

"Oh look," Courtney purred. "It's my two favorite people."

Courtney gave Ty a chaste kiss on the cheek before turning to Juliette and taking in the dress.

"Wow," she said unenthusiastically. "That dress is really something."

"It was a gift," Juliette said and Ty's brow line darkened. Okay, so maybe he hadn't been the one to send her the dress and the unsigned note. But who else could it have been? Courtney?

Courtney gave her one last look before dismissing her completely. Instead, she leaned into Ty's chest and whispered something in his ear. "Daddy says it's time," was all Juliette caught. *What could that possibly mean?*

Ty nodded and let Courtney drag him over to her father, who was in deep conversation with the small orchestra.

The song they were playing faded to silence as Governor Anderson stepped on stage and took the mic. Courtney and Tyler followed him.

"Good evening, ladies and gentleman. I'd like to thank you all for joining us this evening." The governor paused at a soft round of applause. "This night is incredibly special to me. Not only do we have the opportunity to support the expansion efforts of an incredible charity that is near and dear to my family's heart, but because I also have the opportunity to leak a bit of personal information with you tonight. Many of you know that I have been a very vocal supporter of Senator Chase and his re-election campaign."

Anderson extended a long arm in Tyler's direction and another handful of applause broke out.

"The Senator, like many of us, has officially been initiated into D.C. politics. Yesterday he became the subject of some very disturbing rumors. Rumors that I know wholeheartedly to be untrue. Many of us in this room have been the victim of libelous slander, false accusations, and half-truths thrown about by the media. So don't take it personally, son. You have a calling to serve the greater good of this nation. God will not abandon you on your journey." He smiled at Tyler and Ty nodded in response. Courtney reached out and took his hand in hers and gave it a tight squeeze. Standing on the stage, the three of them looked a bit like a campaign postcard. The almighty governor and his real-life Barbie and Ken.

Ty was practically glowing as he smiled back at Courtney and they shared a knowing look. Then he glanced out into the crowd, all smiles and dimples. His mask only lifted for a millisecond when his blue eyes met hers.

Juliette couldn't look away, her eyes were locked on his as she listened to the governor ramble on.

"So tonight I am proud to give my five hundred closest friends an Anderson exclusive. Because I am not only celebrating Tyler Chase the candidate, but I am also celebrating a new son-in-law. Tyler, I am so thrilled to have such a fine young man and brilliant political mind joining my family and taking my daughter's hand in marriage."

Chapter 19:

Whatever it Takes

The world stopped spinning.

At least that was what it felt like when Governor Anderson dropped his bombshell announcement. The clapping and cheering was muted beneath the racing of her own heart. Governor Anderson pulled Tyler into a tight embrace. Tyler gave the man a genuine hug before spinning around and pulling Courtney into an overly dramatic embrace. Tyler dipped his fiance low and kissed her deep on the lips before standing again.

Juliette watched the two of them, laughing and grinning as if everything in the world was perfect, and wanted to throw up. Maybe it was perfect. Courtney was happy. Or at least she certainly seemed that way. And making it official meant that Tyler might actually have abandoned his pursuit of her. So what if her heart ached and her stomach clenched at the thought of the two of them married? This was what she wanted, for Ty to let go and move on.

But you never considered marriage.

That had been a stupid oversight on her part and now she was going to have to live with her mistake. But she couldn't be happy tonight. Tonight she was going to be sick.

Juliette melted into the crowd, inching her way to the nearest exit. She would not pass out in front of five hundred D.C. elites. Nor would she throw up in this magnificent gown. She would be miserable and self-pitying in her own apartment behind closed doors, like every other decent person in this city.

Juliette marched through the entrance and down the steps, her eyes focused only on the coat check.

Crap. She didn't have the ticket. Covington did.

"Leaving so soon?" he said, and she turned to find Covington standing in the alcove nearby. Talk about someone who had an unnerving way of showing up whenever you thought his name.

"I'm not feeling well. I think it was the champagne," Juliette lied.

Covington nodded and reached into the suit pocket. He pulled out the white ticket stub and handed it to her.

"I have to admit. I had my doubts. But it looks like you're managing all right with your assignment?" His voice rose as if asking a question instead of making a statement.

Juliette muttered, "Yes," before handing the attendant the ticket for their coats.

Covington took a step closer and placed a single finger on the bottom of her chin. He tilted her head upward so that she had nowhere to look but his eyes, which were a stormy gray.

"You have a tendency to step into the shadows, hiding yourself away when you get nervous or scared. A good grifter knows that confidence is everything. Never let anyone make you feel as if you don't belong. And even if you do feel that way, never, ever, show it."

She nodded again and he frowned. "Yes, sir." she said with more authority. "I hear what you're saying."

"Good." Covington grabbed their coats from the attendant and placed them on the counter. Then, as if she couldn't master the art of dressing herself, he held out her wool and fur coat and she slipped her arms inside. He turned her to face him full on. As he fastened the drawstring tight around her waist she saw Tyler. The senator was standing at the peak of the stairs, watching them. There was something puzzling about his expression. It wasn't concern, but something darker. Anger or jealousy, perhaps?

Well, good. Now he knows what it feels like.

Covington surprised her by putting on his own coat and nudging her gently to the door.

"You're leaving too?"

"But of course. I wouldn't imagine sending a young attractive woman like yourself out into the city alone. What kind of gentleman would I be if I didn't at least see you to your door?"

"That's very kind, but not necessary."

Covington held open the door and for a split second she thought she saw his gaze drift off behind them. It lasted only for an instant and then his attention centered entirely on Juliette. She declined the escort--up until the black limo pulled up to the curb and the driver stepped out to assist them. Suddenly she didn't see the harm in accepting a ride from her employer. After all, what's the worst that could happen?

You could end up dead and buried at the bottom of some construction site.

Right. Well, plenty could happen if she trusted the likes of Dean Covington, but she was desperate to get away from the happy couple. And Covington, like some magical fairy godfather, offered the perfect getaway car.

Chapter 20: House Call

Covington was nothing but polite as they drove to her apartment. They talked of the weather, of D.C. politics, and her favorite classes at Georgetown. He was impressed with her GPA and the fact that she was now semi-fluent in French and Russian. "We'll have to get you over to Paris so that you can fine-tune your skills."

She lit up at the thought. Up until now she had been convinced that she blew her chance to get in with Covington. If she failed, there was no way he was going to give her a second shot. But Covington seemed pleased as punch with the recent developments.

The driver slowed as they turned onto her street. Covington pushed a button on the intercom. "Third townhouse to your left, Zeke."

Juliette frowned. "How do you know where I live?"

"I make it my business to know everything about my employees. It's a good rule to live by. Perhaps you should give it a try."

The limo came to a stop and Zeke jumped out to open her door. Covington gave her a swift wave goodbye before disappearing behind the tinted glass window. Even with the distance she could feel Covington's gaze examining her every move. His presence made her hands jittery and she nearly dropped her keys as she worked to open the outer door. Once inside she rushed past the mailboxes and straight to the stairs. She was in desperate need of time to think.

Juliette stepped into the steaming tub of water and the mass of bubbles swished around her ankles. She winced as she lowered herself into the claw-foot tub. At first the water seemed to scorch her skin. After a few moments her body embraced the warmth like a big, fluffy blanket. She sank farther into the bubbles and let her headrest over the edge of the tub.

Juliette had one single objective for the evening: forget everything that had happened during the last forty-eight hours. That had proven a difficult thing to do. After arriving at her apartment she immediately stripped from the dress, washed off her makeup, and donned a pair of sweatpants and a baggy t-shirt. She ordered takeout and sat on the couch, ready to resume her night of trashy TV. But after thirty minutes she found she couldn't sit still. Her mind wouldn't focus on what was happening on TV.

She opened a bottle of wine, hoping that would force her to relax, but she drank the first glass in less than three minutes and found herself pouring another one in five.

Finally she settled on taking a long, hot bath. She turned off the light, lit a few lavender-scented candles along the sink, and filled the tub with her favorite bubble bath. Her iPod was nestled in the corner, playing her favorite Coldplay tunes. Sure, she was still carrying around her bottle of wine, but she hadn't yet resorted to drinking straight from the bottle, so she considered this an improvement.

And for the moment it appeared to be working. She felt the tension ease out of her as she closed her eyes and shut out the world. The music was like her mood, gray and melancholy, and it made her feel welcomed. Perhaps misery really did love company?

Juliette woke up with a start. The water was ice-cold, the bubbles were long gone, and her phone was vibrating instead of ringing. She pulled herself out of the tub and wrapped a towel beneath her arms. She patted her hands frantically against the cotton before answering the phone. When she swiped the screen, she saw Tyler Chase's name.

So not what she wanted to see.

She hit ignore and switched the phone to airplane mode. And just like that, the outside world was completely cut off.

Juliette grabbed the half empty bottle of wine and headed to her bedroom. She toweled off, slipped into her third pair of yoga sweats for the day and another long-sleeved t-shirt. She stared at herself in the mirror. It was a far cry from the girl she had seen earlier this evening. The one who looked like she donned the cover of Vogue or Esquire for Men. Now she was just plain old Juliette Morgan.

There's nothing wrong with that, a voice told her, and she was inclined to agree. She climbed into bed, grabbed the book on her nightstand, and settled in for the night.

Juliette jerked awake for the second time that evening. Only this time it was the pounding on her apartment door that woke her.

She glanced at the alarm clock, which read 2:23. "You have got to be kidding me." She had only been asleep for an hour.

Juliette tried to ignore the knocking but her curiosity got the better of her. If she had been a betting woman she would have put money on one Mr. Tyler Chase, though there was also a slim chance it might be Courtney. Juliette wasn't in a hurry to see either one of them. The door rattled again as someone resumed the knocking.

She pulled herself out of the bed and plodded to the front door.

"I'm coming," she snapped at what had to be the sixth set of pounding. *Don't these people know I have neighbors?*

She stood on her tiptoes so that she could peek through the peephole. It wasn't Ty or Courtney. It was Winston. The friend slash assistant slash campaign advisor.

He pounded again and she jerked backward. *Holy hell. This was ridiculous.*

Juliette undid the locks and yanked the door open before pulling him inside and closing it again.

"What the hell is wrong with you?"

"Huh?" He looked completely perplexed.

"It's two-thirty in the morning. I have neighbors, you know."

"Oh, yeah. They're not home. Well, Gina and Mike aren't anyway. And the old couple can't hear a thing without their hearing aids. Dead to the world, they are."

"That doesn't make it okay to pound on people's doors in the middle of the night." Juliette crossed her arms over her chest and glared at him.

"Riiiight" he said. "I'm sorry?"

The fact that he said it like a question was an obvious sign that he wasn't sorry at all. Clearly he didn't understand what he had done wrong.

"What are you doing here?"

His face suddenly lit up again as he remembered his reason for banging on her door.

"I came to get you."

"To get me? For what?"

"There's something you need to see." Winston grabbed her arm and pulled her to the door.

"Hold on." She stumbled after him. He turned at her resistance.

"What is it?"

"I'm not even dressed and I haven't agreed to go anywhere with you. I don't even know you."

"You know Ty."

She waited for him to continue because certainly that wasn't reason enough to leave the comforts of her own living room.

"Just trust me. There's a lot more to this story than meets the eye. You have a right to know the truth. If you come with me, you'll get just that."

"The truth about what?"

"About Ty."

Juliette began to back away. "No. I don't want to know anything more about Ty. In fact, I want nothing to do with him."

Winston's phone rang and he snapped it open. "Hello?"

Juliette took advantage of the distraction to move farther into the living room. She didn't want to go anywhere with Winston. He could tell her whatever it was she needed to know right there.

Winston turned away from her. His voice dipped lower. *Who was he talking to and why was he trying to keep it a secret?* Juliette tried to listen in on his conversation. But the voice on the other end was muffled and Winston was only offering vague answers to the conversation.

"Winston?" she called and he jerked around at the sound of her voice. "Who is it?"

"Nothing," he mouthed and into the phone he said, "I have to go." He snapped the phone shut and turned to the door.

"You're leaving?"

"Yeah. I've got something to take care of. You know how politics is. No rest for the weary when you're on the campaign trail."

He pulled open the door and stepped into the hallway, shutting it behind him before she even had a chance to say goodbye.

Chapter 21: The Fallout

Juliette spent the morning coming up with creative ways that she could bail on her lunch date with Courtney. She wasn't ready to face Ty's new fiancé. It was cruel and unusual punishment, really. And yet, she couldn't afford to let on that the engagement bothered her.

Not that it made her feel any better about her current situation. So she finally gave in and resorted to the age old excuse of, "I'm sick." *That darn twenty-four hour flu bug was a real bitch.* Thankfully, when she called Courtney to cancel she got her voicemail. The girl hadn't called back yet--another small miracle.

Then Juliette resorted to her godmother's tried-and-true cure for heartache: baking. She lined up a row of art deco canisters on the counter: Flour, sugar, baking powder, baking soda, and cocoa. Then she pulled out her roommate's bulky stand mixer. Margaret never minded when she borrowed her things. Especially if the end result was sinfully delicious eats.

She made cupcakes first. Two dozen chocolate and white with butter cream frosting and sprinkles. Then she started on the brownies. She didn't know what she's d do with all these goodies. Perhaps hold a bake sale so she could make rent after Covington fired her. And he had just commented on how good she was doing. But she wasn't doing well at all. She couldn't stand to be in the same room as Courtney.

There was a knock at her door. Juliette froze, batter covered spatula in midair. Was that Courtney? Had she come to check on her? What was she going to say?

Juliette carefully balanced the spoon on the edge of the batter bowl and wiped her flour covered hands on the faded apron. She really needed to move to an apartment with better security. Maybe a street-level intercom that required uninvited guests to be buzzed into the building.

Juliette didn't bother looking through the peephole. It had not once prevented her from opening the door and coming face to face with her mysterious visitors. Plus she didn't want to get flour all over the back of the door. So she used the clean edge of her apron to turn the knob.

"Can I come in?" Tyler asked and her heart fell through her stomach. Her eyes drifted down the hallway for other onlookers. Sure, she lived in a converted townhouse with few neighbors, but it didn't mean someone wouldn't spot the senator. All she needed was another story about their alleged affair.

It's only alleged because they haven't proven it yet.

Right.

Juliette stepped aside and Ty crossed the threshold. He took the door from her and closed it gently behind him.

"Look," Juliette started. "If this is about last night, I already told Winston I'm not interested."

"What? Winston was here last night?"

So he hadn't known. Which meant he most likely was not the mystery caller on the other end of the phone.

"Yeah, he came by for a few minutes. You didn't send him?"

"No. I did not."

"Fine. Then why did you come here?"

"I thought that we should talk, you know. About the engagement."

Juliette laughed. It came out bitter. "You think I want to talk about it? I have nothing to say. And it doesn't really matter what I think, does it?"

"That's not fair. You told me you weren't interested. I said I would leave Courtney and you practically demanded that I keep the relationship going."

"Well, I didn't mean you should marry the girl."

"I did what was necessary to keep the peace. I thought you'd be happy since you've become so invested in my political future."

The timer on the oven dinged and Juliette turned to retrieve her cookies. She set the tray on top of the stove and let the oven door slam shut.

Ty reached for one of the cupcakes and she swatted his hand away with her dish towel. "Don't you dare."

"Are you planning on eating four-and-a-half dozen baked goods in the next twenty-four hours?"

"Baking helps me stay calm. You, on the other hand, bring me nothing but stress. And if you keep popping in and out of my life I am going to be making baked goods for the next ten years."

"Come on, it's not that bad."

Juliette stared at him. He really had no idea. The way she felt when she was with him. The way her body relaxed at his touch, the way her heart leapt every time she stared into those deep blue eyes. He was her Achilles heel and he was destroying her one breathtaking kiss at a time.

"Do you love her?" Suddenly Juliette wanted to know.

Tyler was silent as he stared back at her.

"You do love her, right, Ty?"

"I only love one woman." He moved a step closer and warning bells went off in her head. *This is how it starts. If he gets less than six inches away, you're a goner.*

She stepped back against the counter and searched for a distraction. She grabbed the nearest cupcake and held it out in front of him.

"Here."

"I can have one?" he asked.

"Yes, but you need to leave now."

"What if I don't want to leave?"

She sighed loudly. "I don't really care what you want, Tyler. What if someone saw you come here? It's not that hard to figure out who I am. If they put two and two together and the story of your cheating rears its ugly head again"

"So what?" He pulled the liner from the bottom of the cupcake. "I lose the election. I don't get married. Name one bad thing that comes out of all of it."

"How about my face all over the nation's largest newspapers. I'll be branded as that whore who broke up your engagement. It never turns out well for the other woman."

"You aren't the other woman," he muttered into the cupcake. "You're the woman."

He took a bite and chewed without taking his eyes off her. She stopped breathing as she watched him, wanting his words to be true. But if there was one thing she was certain of, it was that Tyler Chase was an excellent liar.

"If you don't love her, than maybe you should tell her that."

"Why are you so worried about Courtney?"

"Because she's my friend."

His laugh was a bitter slap in the face. "You've known her for what--a few weeks?"

"Nearly two months." It didn't sound any more impressive and she almost wished she hadn't said anything at all. She was making his case for him. "And who cares how long I've known her. The point is that I think she's a good person--a decent person. She doesn't deserve a cheating fiancé; who doesn't love her and is only using her for political gain."

"And what are you using her for?"

"Excuse me?"

He set the half-eaten cupcake on the counter. "I think it's a huge coincidence that the day after we slept together you have the sudden desire to befriend the woman I'm dating. It's not sane. In fact, it's kind of creepy. Stalker creepy."

"So now I'm a stalker? You're the one that keeps showing up at my doorstep unannounced. How the hell did you people even get my address?"

That shut him up, but only for a second.

"Fine, maybe we've both done some slightly questionable activities in the last few weeks."

That was the understatement of the century.

"But right now, Courtney is content with our original story. Telling her about the affair will only hurt her. I know you think that I'm a complete jerk, but I never meant to hurt her."

"Then why agree to marry her?" Juliette's words flew out at him like daggers. He instinctively took a step back.

"It's complicated. But please believe me when I say that no one is going into this agreement blind."

"Agreement? You're getting married not selling off a company."

"Courtney wants this, which means her father wants this. My goal is to make him happy. At least until the election."

Juliette picked at the tray of cookies in front of her. She busied herself with transferring the warm cookies onto the wire cooling rack. Anything to keep from looking at Tyler.

"You can't say anything," he continued. "Courtney is as complicated as it gets. Not everyone can handle her the way I can."

"Handle?"

"Think of her as a live grenade. There are ways to safely contain the explosion but it has to be done under the right conditions."

"Fine. I won't say anything. But this thing between the two of us is over. And that means no showing up at my doorstep day and night looking all sinful and delicious."

"You think I'm delicious?"

Juliette grabbed his jacket and dragged him to the door. "Did I say delicious? I meant to say, disgusting and pathetic." She jerked the door open. "You need to leave. Now."

He gave her one long, wistful glance before parting. That same look of longing that left her heart aching for more.

Chapter 22: Good Intentions

That night Juliette tossed and turned as she found herself trapped in a nightmare featuring Courtney and Ty. The perfect political couple, announcing their wedding and walking down the aisle in a magnificent Catholic church the size of a small palace. She dreamed of Courtney beaming in a beautiful white dress. She dreamed that Courtney designated her as maid of honor. And then right when the minister asked if there were any objections to the wedding, a voice from the back of the chapel would cry out, "I object!" The words boomed off the stained glass windows and gilded chandeliers. All eyes turned toward Juliette and the guests screamed out at her. Traitor! Whore! Harlot!

It was the same dream over and over and each time she woke in a drenched sweat.

The third time she climbed out of bed and padded into the living room, swiping another cookie from the countertop as she went. She settled down into the sofa and clicked on the TV. Then she began mindlessly flicking through the channels, searching for a distraction.

She found herself nervously reaching for her phone and scanning her emails. She was so miserable she wanted to text Courtney right now and confess. She didn't care what she had promised Ty. Their lies had gone too far. And what if Courtney found out the truth before she finished her assignment? It would devastate their friendship and she would have to explain to Covington why she shouldn't go within a twenty-foot radius of her mark.

She set the phone down. Tyler was right. Courtney was going to be upset either way. If she told her the truth now it would only make things worse.

Another ten minutes crept by. Juliette was groggy and tired, but she didn't want to have that same dream for a fourth time. The sugar failed to keep her awake. She headed to the kitchen to grab a fresh bottle of wine. Her eyes lingered on the liquor cabinet. *Maybe this is an occasion for something a little stronger?*

She set the wine bottle down and opened the cupboard door. She scanned the clear bottles until her hand stopped in front of an unopened bottle of tequila. That would be perfect.

She grabbed it by the neck, moved back to the fridge to grab a lemon and then reached for a salt shaker near the stove. She carried her ensemble to the coffee table and got to work. Fifteen minutes and two shots later she was already feeling a little tipsy. She sat sprawled out on the living room floor surfing YouTube videos.

Her computer chimed and a bubble popped up on the corner of the window. It was an instant message from Margaret.

Margs2.0: Hey fabulous bitch. What are you doing up so late?

Jules2381: I could ask you the same thing.

Juliette was pretty certain she misspelled a few of those words.

Margs2.0: Not that late. I'm three hours behind you, remember?

Jules2381: yeps.

She wanted to say more but the typing required too much brain power.

Jules2381: Turn on your webcam. I don't want to type anymore. Too much work.

Margaret agreed and in less than ten seconds she received a request to share video with her roommate.

Her bright face and bushy brown hair immediately filled the screen.

"Hey beautiful," she said and then frowned. "What the hell are you wearing?"

Juliette looked down at her shirt. It had a giant pink Care Bear on it standing in front of a rainbow. She had bought it on a whim one day, liking the retro feel. But she had never had the courage to wear it in public. With her roommate gone, she had pulled out the shirt from the back of her closet and clung to it like a five-year-old with a security blanket. It didn't help that there was a chocolate stain over her left boob.

"It's been a rough day," Juliette shrugged.

Margaret squinted at the monitor. "Is that tequila?"

"Yes, would you like to do a virtual shot with me?"

"Sure, but only if you promise to tell me what's really going on."

Juliette licked the salt off the back of her hand, lifted the shot glass to her lips, and tipped her head back. The liquor burned as it moved down her throat. She winced at the sour taste as she sucked on another lemon wedge. Then she tossed the rind into the glass before glancing back up at her friend. "What do you want to know?"

"How about you start at the beginning?" Margaret reappeared with her own bottle of alcohol, El Toro, Juliette was guessing from the little red sombrero shaped lid.

So that's exactly what Juliette did. She told Margs everything. Well, everything having to do with Tyler Chase and the secret affair. And it was a relief to get it all off her chest. By the time she was finished she had polished off more than a half dozen shots and Margs was not far behind. And instead of making her tired, the liquor seemed to have the opposite effect. She was ready to throw caution to the wind. To do something completely and totally crazy. And she could do that, because it was only--she glanced at the clock--three a.m.

"I think you should tell her everything," Margaret said, surprising the hell out of Juliette. "Why should some slick politician get to jerk you around and then beg and plead that you keep his dirty little secrets so that he doesn't ruin his chances at re-election?"

"It's not like I didn't have a say in the matter. I was kind of a willing participant. I mean, I'm the cheating whore in this equation."

"Oh for God's sake, stop with the guilt trip. He didn't tell you he was involved with someone when you first met. That's his fault not yours. And the motel, well, any red-blooded woman is going to react to someone all dreamy and naked in bed with them. It was like he was setting you up to fail so that you would feel too guilty to challenge him on this."

Juliette slammed her hand down on the coffee table and Margaret jumped on the other side of the computer screen.

"You are so effing right," Juliette declared. "It *was* his fault. And Courtney *totally* needs to know what a lying ass he is. I'm going to call her and tell her right now." Juliette scanned the space around her. "Where the hell is my phone?"

She ran her hands over the sofa cushions, lifted the tasseled pillows, she even bent over and peeked under the couch, but her phone was nowhere to be found.

"Okay, so maybe tomorrow then."

"Tomorrow's no good. You'll just back out of it if I'm not around."

"Unless you've got a spare phone I can use, it's not going to happen tonight."

"So write her an email."

Juliette laughed again. "I could barely type two hours ago. I'm pretty sure my spell check would implode."

Margaret clapped her hands and began bouncing up and down on her knees. She lifted the laptop closer, the webcam zoomed in on her face. "Make a video! Like one of those secret confessions they post on that site My Dirty Little Secrets."

Juliette considered it for a moment. A video sounded fun but there was no way in hell she would ever post a confession online.

"You don't have to post it publicly. You can make a private video. It gets sent from the website directly to whoever you want to see it."

And for some reason, at that exact moment in time, Juliette figured the idea of a video confession was a fantastic one. And she recorded a thirty-second confession with her webcam, just before passing out on the sofa.

Chapter 23: Gone Wrong

Juliette woke with a roaring headache and a crick in her neck from sleeping with her head on the couch arm. She winced as she surveyed the damage to her apartment. The laptop computer had gone into standby mode and her roommate was long gone, but the evidence of their virtual tequila fest was still present. The previously full bottle was now empty. Multiple shot glasses lined the table and lemon wedges were scattered across the hardwood floors.

"Oh my God."

She stared at the laptop as if it were going to come to life and eat her. It wasn't like in the movies, where you get drunk and can't remember anything that happened the night before. As she stared at the blackened monitor she remembered everything--the confession to her friend, the overwhelming guilt she was attempting to chase away with hard liquor. But most of all she remembered the video confession she sent to Courtney.

Juliette jabbed the power button and her computer roared to life. She didn't have to click very far to find what she was looking for. The still open window showed a confirmation message, stating her video confession had been mailed to C.Anderson32@gwu.edu.

Holy crap.

Juliette went to her own email, expecting some irate message from her friend. But there was nothing there. Then she jumped up and scanned the area for her phone. Where the hell was it?

She raced to her bedroom and found the phone sitting on her nightstand, but when she picked it up she saw that there were no missed calls or texts. She also saw that it was only 6:45 a.m. Courtney didn't have her first class until ten. There was a good chance she wasn't even up yet.

Juliette grabbed her phone, jacket, and keys. She slipped into a pair of ballet flats and ran out the door, dialing Ty's number as she charged down the steps. A decision she later regretted. Apparently there was still plenty of liquor floating around in her system. She nearly tripped and would have fallen down the last three steps if it hadn't been for her death grip on the handrail.

Ty didn't answer after the first four rings and the voicemail clicked on. She didn't leave a message.

They didn't need any more incriminating evidence of their relationship. Come to think of it, maybe they should get burner phones. Those were supposed to be untraceable, right?

She shook her head and dialed a cab company instead. She needed a ride and at this hour she wasn't likely to find a taxi on the streets near her apartment. Once that was done, she redialed Ty. Twice. The third time she gave in. "Ty, it's me. Meet me at Courtney's place, ASAP."

She hoped to God he would get the message in time. She needed to warn him about what might happen. Then she had a horrible thought. What if Ty was already at Courtney's s? They were engaged, after all, it wasn't completely out of the question.

A cab pulled up and she climbed inside and gave him the address. Thankfully the ride to GWU would cost less than five bucks. She was running through cash almost as fast as she was running through lies.

Her phone buzzed just as she was pacing back and forth in front of the entrance to Courtney's apartment. Now that she was here, she had absolutely no idea what to say. How did she explain the odd hour of her visit? How did she keep Courtney from checking her email? Or even better, how could she get rid of it before Courtney even discovered it in her inbox?

"Hello?"

Tyler's concerned voice greeted her. "What's wrong? Are you okay?" He genuinely sounded worried. About her. Though it could have been about the fact that her voicemail had said she was headed to Courtney's apartment.

"I'm fine. For the moment. Things might take a turn for the worse in a few minutes."

"I don't understand. What are you doing at Courtney's place? She's downtown with me."

The immediate tension drained from her chest and shoulders. At least now she didn't have to deal with Courtney face-to-face.

"I did something stupid, Ty, and now I need your help."

He paused for a moment. "Anything."

"I need you to distract Courtney."

"She's still sleeping, so that shouldn't be a problem."

"Perfect. Grab her phone and hide your computer. If she wakes up I need you to keep her offline and away from any email."

"I don't understand. What's happened?"

"Look, if you want to save your fake engagement you need to do exactly as I say. Right now."

Tyler was quiet at her verbal threat, but eventually promised to follow her instructions. She hung up before he could ask any more questions. And now that Juliette was certain Courtney's apartment was empty, she needed to find a way inside.

She walked up to the call box and entered the key code to the lobby. Thank God Courtney was too lazy to care about things like security. She was one of those girls who used her pin in front of total strangers, not even aware of who might be looking over her shoulder.

As she stepped into the ritzy, remodeled apartment building she knew why it was so easy for Courtney to be lax about such things. The $4,000 monthly rent tended to keep out the riffraff. And the Archstone did boast claims of round the clock security. Though the night guard at the desk barely glanced at her as she walked by. Who could blame him? There were at least a hundred tenants, maybe more. He probably assumed Juliette belonged here.

Juliette took the elevator to the 12th floor and then headed for Courtney's apartment, 1203. She glanced quickly for any cameras and once satisfied pulled out her tools. She's d been picking locks since she was thirteen and found most entry locks a piece of cake. Slowly she twisted each of the thin rods into the doorknob until she felt the one in her right hand catch. She pulled at the trigger and the lock released. The door crept open. Juliette quickly slipped inside and shut it behind her.

Then she hesitated. *What if Ty was lying and Courtney was here, asleep in her own bed?* But she heard no signs of living, so she stepped farther into the apartment and began searching for Courtney's laptop.

The apartment was impeccable; not a hair was out of place. She moved past the kitchen and dining room into the living room, but there was no sign of the laptop. She headed to the office, secretly wondering what kind of college student had enough money to live in a place with a spare bedroom. Apparently the rich kind with daddy governors who lie and steal and cheat their way to the top.

She didn't have any problem with lying and stealing, clearly. But at least she wasn't trying to hide what she was. Politicians are just crooks with fancy suits and bad hair.

But Ty has great hair.

Yeah, well there's an exception to every rule.

There was no sign of the computer in the office so she headed for Courtney's bedroom. She was just pushing open the door when she heard the front door open.

Juliette froze in mid-step, which in hindsight was stupid.

Then the familiar voice called out her name. "Jules?"

It was Ty. "What are you doing here?" she demanded. "Where is Courtney?"

"Relax. She's sleep and this sounded urgent."

"It will be even more urgent if she walks in on the two of us breaking into her apartment."

"We're not breaking in. Or at least I'm not. I have a key." Ty continued into the bedroom leaving Juliette to follow. As soon as she entered she immediately spotted the Mac Book Pro on the nightstand. It was closed but she could see the small white light that indicated it was still on.

I hope she doesn't use a password protection for the main user account.

Juliette reached for the computer. If she was lucky maybe Courtney was still logged into her email and Juliette wouldn't even have to bother with testing out a billion unique password combinations. *They should have an app for hacking into your best friend's computer.*

Juliette peered down at the computer screen. The last internet browser was still open with at least a dozen or so different tabbed web pages. Unfortunately, Courtney's email account wasn't one of them.

"What are you doing?" Ty leaned against the closet door.

"I did something really, really stupid."

"To her laptop?"

"No." Juliette buried her head in her hands. She couldn't bear to look at him as she admitted what a ridiculously stupid mistake she had made.

He came closer and sat on the other side of the bed. "Look, it can't be that bad. You're probably just overreacting."

"I made a video confession about our sleeping together and emailed it to your fiancé at three in the morning."

Chapter 24:

Ticking Time Bomb

Ty's legs nearly gave out and he slipped off the bed. She reached out to steady him, her hand gripping his toned biceps.

"Why would you do that?" he asked.

The look on his face was enough to make her heart break. "I was angry," she pleaded. "And drunk. Very, very drunk. So I took some rather questionable advice and dealt with the issue head-on. It felt good, at least until I passed out."

"Christ." He pulled his arm away and stood to face her. "What the hell is wrong with you? Why couldn't you just leave it alone?"

"I'm sorry, but yelling at me now Isn't going to get the damn video back."

"And you lurking about over her computer is?"

Juliette slammed the laptop closed and stormed out into the living room. She couldn't think in the bedroom, with pictures of Courtney staring her down at her, calling them both out as dirty little liars.

"You're wasting your time." Ty brushed past her, his cell phone already glued to his ear.

"Unless you have got a better idea, shut the hell up."

He spun around and shot a furious glare her way. "It just so happens, I do."

He turned his attention back to the phone. "Winston, it's me." He spoke into the phone. "I have a little situation. Call me. Now." He clicked "end" and shoved the phone back into his coat pocket.

"Unless Winston is a computer hacker, we're screwed."

Ty was silent.

"Oh my God. He *is* a computer hacker."

"I didn't say that."

"Yeah, but you didn't deny it either." She thought for a moment. "Is that how the two of you managed to find my home address?"

"No. Your address is in the student directory. Publicly available and everything."

"No, Margaret's address is in the directory. Mine is anonymous."

His phone rang and he immediately began explaining the situation to whom Juliette could only hope was Winston. After a few minutes the two men hung up and Ty pulled the laptop away from Juliette and tucked it under his arm.

"He's expecting us. The sooner he gets this computer the better."

"If he's such a good computer hacker, why do we need to go to him? Can't he break into her email remotely?"

"Sure, if we had hours. But we don't. The fastest way into anything is always direct, through the source."

"You sound like you do this for a living," Juliette said.

He smiled. "And you sound like you're intrigued."

"I am."

Ty opened the door and they headed into the hallway. Once he had locked the front door they started for the elevator.

"Hacking is one of those things that seems like magic, to me. I mean, I get that it's a science; everything is basically a series of zeroes and ones, right? So it's only a matter of being smarter than the person who designed the program."

"Something like that," he said. The elevator doors opened into the lobby and Juliette headed towards the front entrance. Ty grabbed her arm and spun her in the opposite direction. They moved behind the bay of elevators and into a hallway.

She followed him. "Where are we going?"

"I drove here. My car's in the garage."

He pushed the door open and headed for the illegally parked Mercedes with chrome detailing. He clicked off the alarm and opened her door, but just as she turned to step inside she heard the sound of shattering glass.

Ty fell to the ground and Juliette jumped inside the car without thinking. She dropped the laptop on the floor and reached for the door behind her. The attacker grabbed for her but he was too slow. She smashed his hand between the door and when it bounced open he fell backward, crying out in pain. She slammed the car door shut a second time, only before she could click the locks the driver's side door opened. *Oh God! Someone else is climbing inside!*

Juliette panicked. Where the hell was her purse? She always, always, always had a weapon in her purse.

She grabbed the bag and was immediately grateful it didn't have a zipper. She dumped the contents all over the floor and found what she needed. Her fingers clasped around the worn leather handle of Jean's knife. Sure, most girls carried pepper spray, but she found the threat of the knife was a more effective deterrent. It only took one swing for her attacker to realize that she actually knew what she was doing.

The man crawled over her. Juliette waited until he was within arm's distance and swung. The knife slashed across his face. A thick line of blood swelled over his cheek.

"You stupid little bitch." He threw a heavy punch at her and the knife slipped from her fingers.

He took another swing at her and she tried to scramble out of the way but with the car door closed there was nowhere to go. His fist collided with her stomach, knocking all the air out of her lungs. The pain was excruciating and for a moment it was all she could think about. Then she felt his hands crawling up her legs. He gripped her tightly as he pulled her body toward him. She threw her hands above her head, searching for anything she could grab on to.

Her nails scratched at the leather interior of the door. Just as she managed to wrap her left hand on a door handle the attacker disappeared.

She pulled herself up to see Ty dragging the guy out by his waist. The guy remained immobile, caught by surprise, at least until he was able to clutch at the ground with his feet and get his bearing. He swung at Ty, but Ty was ready. Tyler grabbed a fistful of greasy black curls, and slammed the man's head into the edge of the car. This time the man dropped to the ground and didn't budge. Ty kicked him aside and climbed back into the Mercedes.

"What the hell just happened?" Juliette asked.

"Looks like someone just tried to carjack us." Ty pulled down the mirror and wiped the blood from his forehead. He had a pretty nasty cut near his hairline. "Are you okay?"

Juliette ignored his question. "We should get you to a hospital, you might need stitches."

"Not a chance in hell." He reached into the backseat and grabbed a towel from his gym bag. Then he began tending to the wound. "If we go to a hospital it will be all over the news in a matter of minutes. I don't want the extra attention."

"I thought all press was good press."

"It is, most of the time," he said. "But the key is to know what the story is before you alert the press. I can't do that until I know who attacked me and why."

"How do you know it wasn't a random attack? Did you make some deal with a mob boss or something?"

He grinned. "In my line of work, you never can tell."

There was a knock on the door and the both of them jumped. It wasn't the apartment manager, or the night guard, both of whom had reason to be monitoring the security feed in the parking garage. Rather it was a little old woman still dressed in her pajamas, a fuzzy red robe covering her blue and white nightgown. She had a pair of heavy boots on her feet, which looked extremely out of place.

Ty rolled down the window.

"I called the cops the moment I heard the screaming. Are you two okay?"

And just like that their plans to keep the attack quiet evaporated into thin air.

Chapter 25:

Media Frenzy Take One

Within ten minutes a half dozen police cars arrived, along with two TV crews from local stations and Winston, who apparently also monitored the police scanners in his free time. "You'd d be amazed at all the relevant breaking news we pick up simply by monitoring a few key channels." He told her jokingly as he climbed out of his own car.

Actually, she wasn't. She knew it was the same trick that the news crews used to get the drop on breaking news.

Winston strolled over to the small crowd of detectives and paramedics now doting over Ty and Juliette in tandem. "Sorry, guys. I need to speak with the senator in private for second. I promise it won't take long."

"We're not finished questioning him," the first detective said. He was a tall, heavyset man with a bald spot on the dead center of his head. He was dressed in a wrinkled gray suit that paled in comparison to anything that Ty or Winston would ever wear. But then again, the detective was at a much lower pay grade. Or he just didn't give a damn.

Winston gave one of those charming smiles and then nudged Ty away from the group. They made it all the way to the garage elevator before he stopped and the two began exchanging words. Juliette could tell by the look in Ty's eyes that he was concerned about something Winston had just said. For a split second his shoulders tensed and his brow creased. But as soon as he spotted Juliette watching him it vanished.

They continued talking until the detective strode over. "We really need to finish getting a statement."

Ty and Winston split up and Winston moved on to her. "Where's the laptop?"

"What?" she said.

"Courtney's computer. Where is it?"

In all the commotion Juliette had completely forgotten about the whole reason they were there. Juliette pointed to the car. The shiny computer was on the floor of the passenger seat.

Winston moved like a stealthy fly, weaving in and out between clusters of people until he was on the other side of the car. He pulled open the door and grabbed the laptop then slipped it into his messenger bag. The door was closed before the nearest officer bothered to ask what he was doing.

"Just checking for Mr. Chase's keys. He thought he dropped them during the attack but I don't see them."

"One of the officers might have grabbed them," the officer said before turning to the other uniformed cop and inquiring about the keys. Meanwhile Winston moved back to Juliette.

"Who the hell are you?" she asked.

"One day, I'll be happy to answer all your questions but I am afraid now is not the time. I need to get you out of here before--"

"Oh my God. Tyler, are you all right?" Courtney's cool voice rang out through the garage.

"Never mind," Winston said as he shot a look at Courtney. "If she asks, the two of you were attempting to plan a surprise engagement dinner. Make sure she knows that it was a secret, that Ty asked you not to tell."

"Okay," Juliette said. "What about the computer? We still haven't gotten the video yet."

"I'm on it. I'll try to finish with it before she notices."

Juliette nodded.

Courtney had already cornered Ty and was inspecting his forehead as if she was a trained paramedic. Juliette rose, planning on greeting her, but the moment she stood the world began to spin. Winston grabbed her and eased her back down.

"Can we get a paramedic over here?" he yelled.

"No, I'm fine, just a little shaken up is all."

"Ty says the guy hit you pretty hard. You may have internal injuries."

"I do not have internal injuries. It was one punch and it caught me off guard. I'll be fine with a few Tylenol and some ice."

But it was too late. The paramedic came over along with Ty and Courtney. The whole group was suddenly talking around her, asking questions and theorizing what injuries she might have. Courtney even brought up the diabetes, asking the paramedics if they should be more concerned about her injuries as a result. Before she knew it the paramedics had whisked her into an ambulance. She played along, though she flat-out refused to be strapped down on the stretcher. Tyler, Winston, and Courtney followed the ambulance and met her at GWU Hospital. Then they began an endless--and in her honest opinion pointless--trek of x-rays and scans.

In the end they determined that she had two bruised ribs, but no broken bones or critical injuries. Though she would have a nasty black and green bruise on her chest. They offered to keep her overnight for observation, but Juliette was certain they were only extending the courtesy to please her high-profile escort and his entourage, so she declined. Then the three of them argued about who should drive Juliette home. Winston finally won out with a *don't even think about questioning me* look.

Ty gave up and went off with Courtney.

Winston brought the car around to the front entrance of the hospital. Juliette climbed inside, very careful not to put pressure on her right side. Once he checked to make sure her seatbelt was fastened, he gently closed the door and climbed in on the other side. He started the car and drove down the street two blocks before turning into a second parking lot and pulling the car to a stop.

"What are you doing?"

"We're going to find that stupid video confession of yours right now, before Ty and Courtney get back to his apartment and she thinks to check her email."

Right. All this could have been avoided if she hadn't been piss-ass drunk the night before.

Winston propped the laptop against the steering wheel. It whirled to life and a little chime greeted him as he clicked onto the main page. "What email address did you send it to? The school or a personal account?"

"It's the school one. It was shorter and I didn't have very much hand-eye coordination at the time."

"Right."

He typed in the address for the GWU webpage and then clicked on the log-in button. When it loaded, he typed in Courtney's username. That part was simple. Everyone's username on campus had the same format.

"Is this going to work?" Juliette asked. It wasn't that she didn't trust him. Okay, that was part of it. But she had so much on the line. They all did.

"Well, I can pretty easily remove the email from her account, that way she won't get the link to the video. But because you used an external website to make the video, it means that a third party has a digital copy of your recording on their servers. That will take much more time to hack."

"But you can do it, right? Or is that out of your league?"

Winston stopped typing on the black and white screen. His eyes narrowed as he studied her. She wondered if she had offended him.

"What did Ty tell you?"

"About you? Not much. He said that you were so good at your job because you did a little hacking as a side hobby. You seem to know what you're doing, though. I'm guessing this Isn't a side hobby?"

"Let's just say Ty is my oldest and closest friend. He needed help and I agreed to do so."

"So which is it? You don't run campaigns for a living or you don't hack computers for a living?"

"I'm a freelancer. I do what I want, when I want. Right now, I want my friend to win his senate seat."

He went back to typing away on the computer. After five more minutes he was in Courtney's school account. Juliette pointed to the email in her inbox. "That's it!"

He highlighted it, clicked delete and then opened the trash can and manually removed the backup file. Then he closed the browser and cleared the history. He was just logging out of her account when Juliette's cell phone rang.

"Where are you?" Courtney greeted her. "Ty and I really need to speak with you."

She hesitated. "Why?"

"I think I know who was behind the attack. And more importantly, I've thought of a way for us to one up them."

One up them? What was this, middle school?

"I don't understand."

"Just come back to my place. I'll explain everything there."

Courtney hung up before Juliette could get another word in. She turned to Winston, who was placing the laptop into his black bag. "It sounds as if I am being summoned."

He shrugged. "You don't have to do everything those two say. They don't rule the world. Yet, anyway."

"I could say the same for you."

Winston gave her a sad smile. "I don't do it because I have to, I do it because Ty is my friend, like I said."

"Yeah, well I care about them too."

He gave her a "yeah right" look.

"Okay, fine. I barely know them both. But I do care about Ty. He seems like a great guy. I don't want what happened between us to jeopardize everything he's worked so hard for. Everyone makes mistakes."

Chapter 26: Getting Dirty

Courtney was ready for Juliette the moment she stepped into the apartment. She grabbed Juliette by the arm and dragged her over to the dining room table, which was covered in political propaganda. Posters and flyers, postcards, bumper stickers; there was barely any room left for the bottle of vita-water someone was drinking.

"Here's the thing," she began and Juliette winced. Never had anything good started with the words, *here's the thing*.

"I think the Robertson campaign set us up."

"What?"

Ty shook his head and headed for the kitchen.

"The attack? The convenient charges of an affair? They are doing everything they can to create negative press for this campaign."

Juliette shook her head. "It could have been anyone."

"Please, people don't just randomly get mugged in my parking garage. It's perfectly safe. The only time the police are even called is if a homeless man wanders into the lobby."

Juliette shook her head. "That doesn't mean this is the Robertson campaign at work."

"It doesn't matter if you believe me."

"Then what am I doing here?"

"I want to take a page from their playbook. I want you to infiltrate the enemy."

Juliette heard the crack of a soda can opening and the gentle fizz that followed. She turned to look at Ty in the doorway. He was holding a can of Bud Light. It didn't seem like his beverage of choice. He met her eyes as he raised the can to his lips.

"And what exactly am I supposed to be doing, once I infiltrate this campaign? I'm not going to be able to get close to any important information. They've got plenty of volunteers for the real work. People they already trust, I might add."

Courtney cocked her head to the side. "I don't want you to go in as a volunteer."

Uh oh. What the hell did she want her to do then?

Courtney moved to the table and shuffled some papers around. Then she emerged with a copy of the Washington Post. The very same one with the photo of her and Ty embracing.

"I want you to seduce him."

Juliette nearly fell over. Ty nearly choked on his beer. Apparently this was news to him too.

"What the hell is wrong with you people?" Courtney continued. "It's the perfect idea. Robertson's already tried to attack our campaign by creating a scandal."

"Yeah, but didn't your friend Melissa take that picture? She's not a spy for the Robertson camp."

"There are no friends in politics, Jules. Only well hidden enemies that you have to play nice with."

"So Melissa's not your friend?"

"She sold us out. She took that picture and the moment someone came searching for some dirt and offering a little cash she flipped like an Olympic gymnast on steroids."

It was an odd image, but true, she supposed.

"I don't know, Courtney. I mean, how do you know he'll even fall for it?"

"Oh come on, Jules. You're gorgeous. You've got that curvy innocent brunette look that says, 'I'm the demure little girl next door.' Right, Ty?"

Courtney turned to look at her fiancé; and he fumbled for a moment before nodding in agreement.

"They won't recognize you from the photo, so it's perfect. We put you in as a plant. You work to seduce Robertson. We can mic you and Winston can set up some remote cameras in his office. That way when you finally make your move we can get it all on tape. We can leak the sex tape right before the election."

"Excuse me? Did you just say sex tape? Because I am not having sex with Robertson just so you two can win an election."

"Yeah." Ty's tone morphed from slightly amused to disgusted.

"He attacked you!" Courtney snapped. "He invaded your privacy. If you don't find a new game plan right now, he is going to crush us in the election."

"You don't know that. You don't know anything." Ty slammed the can down on the counter and wiped the wetness from his mouth with the back of his sleeve. You're just jumping to conclusions and assuming that this attack was his handiwork. I'm not sure he's even man enough to do something so devious."

"Oh it's not that devious. You guys only have a few bumps and bruises."

Juliette stepped in between the two of them, arms in the air, pleading for peace.

"A compromise, I think, for good measure." She paused to make certain the two of them were listening. "What if I do infiltrate the campaign and try to dig up some dirt on Robertson without sleeping with the man? Maybe I can get you an inside look at their campaign strategy, or give you all a heads-up about any intel he may have gathered on Tyler."

Courtney crossed her arms over her chest as she pondered the situation. It wasn't exactly what she had wanted. But it was all Juliette was willing to give. Juliette just hoped it was better than nothing.

"Fine. You get in. You find us some good intel. But I swear to God, if that doesn't produce any decent results in three days, we're doing things my way."

Courtney tossed down the newspaper clipping on an empty chair and began organizing the mass of political swag on the table into orderly piles.

Ty came closer. "You sure you want to do this?" he asked. "You don't owe me anything."

Of course she didn't owe him anything. If anything he owed her. He was the one who forgot to mention his girlfriend, now fiancé, when they first met. He was the one ruining her chances with Covington.

"Relax. I can work my way into Robertson's circle."

Chapter 27: Progress Report

Three days later Juliette had made little progress and Courtney was getting antsy. Juliette encouraged her to be patient. To think of it as the calm before the storm. Which would have made for a good analogy, except that Juliette had no idea what the storm would look like or when it might arrive.

Juliette was stepping out of the RNC headquarters when she saw the long black limo parked at the curb and a familiar man standing guard. She didn't ask if he was here for her. As soon as Zeke spotted Juliette he stepped aside and opened the back door.

She climbed inside. Covington sat alone the darkness.

"How's my newest intern?" He raised a small silver travel mug to his lips and took a cautious sip as he watched her. Even in the darkness she could see the swirl of steam rise up around his face.

"Things are okay," she said.

"Just okay."

Juliette regretted her choice of words. She wasn't supposed to tell her boss that she was doing an *okay* job. Covington wanted to be reassured that she could handle the job and whatever he planned for Courtney, or the governor, would go down smoothly.

She heard Zeke climb into the driver's seat and start the vehicle. Within seconds they were pulling out into the traffic.

"Where are we going?" She glanced out the window as the scenery passed by.

"Does it matter?

She shrugged. "I guess not."

"Tell me about Courtney. How is she?"

"She's good. Very ambitious. I get the feeling that she likes to win."

He nodded. "Go on."

"I don't know what else to tell you. We've grown close. She trusts me."

"Is that so?"

He said it like a question he already knew the answer to. And of course he did. Anyone who read the Washington Post did. Her fiancé; had been accused of having an affair.

"Was the engagement your idea?"

"No!" she snapped without thinking. Then she tried to downplay her reaction. "I didn't know about the engagement right away, but if she had told me before I would have encouraged her to say no. I don't want the senator to cause her more pain."

"You don't like Senator Chase?"

Of course she liked Tyler Chase. She was damn near in love with the guy. Or could be, if they didn't have enough baggage between them to supply a small army.

"It's not that I don't like him, I just don't trust him."

Covington took another sip of his coffee. "Let me give you a piece of advice. Don't trust anyone."

"Even you?" she asked.

"Especially me. I can teach you what I know. Make you the best grifter in the world. But know this--at the end of the day, if it comes to a choice between you and another con man, always bet on yourself, because the other guy is certainly going to."

Her mouth suddenly felt dry and she was longing for a cold drink to ease the tension. She found herself yearning to fidget under his intense glare. "Never trust anyone. Got it."

"Good. Now, tell me about the senator."

"Chase?"

"Yes."

She was confused. Wasn't Courtney the mark?

"What do you want to know?"

"I want to know about his campaign. Is he confident that he will win? Has he landed any big endorsements?"

"Other than Courtney's father, I'm not sure. They talk like they are going to win. They really believe they have a chance. And they've got me spying on Robertson's camp. I'm not sure I'm going to find anything useful."

"Sure you will. You're a grifter. You should be able to walk into any room, posing as any person, and get key information out of anybody. If Robertson won't give you that information, find someone close to him who will. But get it. There's always dirt to be found."

"Yeah, well if Courtney were in charge she's d have me just create the dirt."

"That works too," Covington said. "As long as you can stay anonymous and people don't track the story back to you."

The limo slowed and came to a stop. The driver was back at the door before she could get a clear look outside. She glanced across the seat at Covington.

"You don't have to get out on my account," he said. "Zeke will see to it you get home safely. I'm afraid I have more work to do, though, or I'd escort you myself."

"Oh there's really no need. I'll be fine on my own."

"Nonsense. You're still recovering from the attack. I won't have you walking about in such a state."

Such a state? She was fine, just a little tender. But Dean was no longer paying her any attention. He stepped past her and climbed out of the car. Zeke shut the door softly behind him and then headed back to the driver's side. Dean disappeared into the glass skyscraper he called home and Juliette couldn't help but think of the first time she met Ty.

The door to the office building opened and a man in dark jeans and a heavy leather jacket strolled out. He stuck out to Juliette not because his attire was different from the lawyers that frequented the building, but because of the nasty cut on his left cheek. She's d recognize that face anywhere. It was the same one that had stared down at her in Ty's car. The same man who had swung a punch at her so hard she had bruised two ribs.

Juliette jerked away from the window for fear he might see her. Which was foolish. The windows were tinted. No one could see in without being pressed up to the glass. Still, she was more than a little relieved when the limo pulled away from the curb and headed toward her apartment. What was this man doing in Dean Covington's law firm?

Chapter 28: Bait

Juliette was too shaken to have Zeke drop her off at her apartment in Georgetown. So instead she had him drive her to the Starbucks down the street from the DNC headquarters. She knew folks for the Robertson campaign were using the office as their DC headquarters. She also knew that no good campaign could function without a decent cup of coffee. One of them was bound to pop in sooner or later. All she had to do was pick the staffer out of the lineup.

Her luck was running high when thirty minutes later Robertson's chief of staff strolled in. He was older than Tyler by at least ten years, with soft gray roots sprinkled throughout his black hair. He was dressed in typical DC fare: black dress pants and a crisp white shirt with pinstripes so subtle it was barely noticeable if you weren't up close. The sky blue tie was loose around his neck as if he had been unable to breathe with it fastened normally.

He strode up to the register, greeted the clerk--who seemed to know him by name--then pulled out a list of orders. There were a half dozen drinks in all and the barista went straight to work. Thankfully it was two in the afternoon. Juliette couldn't imagine trying to fill an order like that during the six to ten coffee rush.

Juliette took advantage of this opportunity to seek a refill, grabbed her glass, and marched over to the register. "Brittany, can I get some fresh coffee to go?" She handed the young girl her mug after twisting off the lid. Then she looked at Jordan Christoff. "That's some order. I thought I had a caffeine problem."

"I wish it was all for me." He smiled. "Gotta keep the troops happy."

"Oh really? What do you do? Oh wait." She held up a perfectly manicured finger in front of his mouth, mere inches away from his lips. She knew he could smell the vanilla spice moisturizer she had just rubbed over her hands.

"Let me guess. You're a lawyer for a non-governmental organization. Something to do with green energy or global warming."

"That's a good guess. But no. Nothing nearly as glamorous."

"That's a bummer. I was hoping you were one of those die-hard do-gooders."

"Nah. Politician," he said. "Though I do work for a Democrat. Does that count?"

Juliette smiled. "Perhaps. Is your candidate one of those hippy-dippy liberals, or one of those--what was Clinton again--New Democrats?"

He laughed. "You got me. He's definitely the latter."

"Figures."

She leaned into him, not touching, but giving the illusion that she needed to be closer. His body instinctively mirrored hers, curving down as if to cocoon her from the outside world.

"So I guess this means I'm not a do-gooder?"

"Not unless you're a card-carrying PETA member."

"Does the World Wildlife Fund count?"

Juliette tilted her head as she considered his question. "Yes. But only because those pandas are so damn cute."

A frenzied barista set the steaming thermos of coffee in front of Juliette and then looked up at her friend. "Your order is coming right up," she said as she turned back to the espresso machine.

Juliette began screwing the lid back onto her travel mug. "I've always been kind of interested in politics, but never quite worked up the nerve to get involved."

He raised an eye. "You must not be from around here."

"Is it that obvious?"

He leaned into the counter. "Not obvious, refreshing. There are so many politicians in this town it can be like hiking through a minefield. Not to mention people become very jaded and cynical after being in the business for a few years."

"You don't seem all that jaded. Maybe you can give me some pointers?"

"I don't know what good it will do, but I'm certainly happy to try. Do you have plans this evening?"

Juliette smiled. "Not a one."

He pulled out a napkin from the counter. "Let's do this old style." She took the napkin and a pen he pulled out from his pocket and jotted down her cell phone number. Just as she slipped the napkin back toward him the barista set his order on the counter. "Sorry about the wait."

"No problem," He reached into his wallet and tossed two bucks into the tip jar before wishing them both a good day.

Chapter 29: Curiosity

Juliette stood at the entrance of her closet, scrutinizing the three dresses hanging in front of her. She really only had two options. The black dress was too revealing for a man she barely knew. Plus she just wore it to the black and white charity ball with Courtney and Ty. And though he had never claimed the gift, some part of her had already labeled the dress as Ty's gown. The look in his eyes when he spotted her in the gown made her think dirty things. She didn't want someone else looking at her with those naughty bedroom eyes.

Juliette scooted the black dress to the side. "And then there were two," she sighed. The sequined red halter dress and the cream-colored lace and chiffon, which she was pretty certain she wore at Margaret's cousin's wedding.

Ugh. She definitely needed to try them on.

She stepped into the red dress and slipped on her silver heels. While she was inspecting herself in the mirror there was a knock at her door.

Great. Just great. She grabbed the hem of the gown so that she could move more freely and shuffled to the door. The sequins rustled against the fabric and she sounded like a muted maraca as she passed through the kitchen. She leaned against the door and snuck a glimpse through the peephole.

Ty stood in her hallway like some kind of sexual genie. Whenever she had an inappropriate thought of him, he seemed to magically appear.

Juliette opened the door.

"Dare I ask what you're doing here? Haven't your little midnight visits caused enough problems already?"

Ty wasn't listening. His eyes were drinking her in from head to toe. He skimmed every covered and not-so-covered inch of her body. Her skin itched for his touch as she watched his face react. She should have taken a step backward, but she didn't want to break the connection. Instead, she wanted to close the distance between them.

She choked down the urge to touch him and pulled away. Ty took her movement as an invitation to come inside.

"What are you doing?" Juliette asked.

"I came to check in on you, see how things were going with Robertson."

"Oh," she tried to keep her voice steady. "Everything's fine. Why, did Courtney tell you something different?"

"Actually, she said you were on the verge of making a breakthrough."

Juliette leaned against the arm of the couch and kicked off one of her heels. "I think Courtney is exaggerating. I've barely seen Robertson, let alone had a chance to get any intel on him. I might as well be bird-watching."

"It's been a while since I've been on a nature trail, but I think you might be a bit overdressed for bird-watching. Where are you headed tonight?"

"Art gallery, I think." She kept her answer vague.

"Really. By yourself?"

Juliette kicked off her other shoe, making her three inches shorter. "What does it matter?"

Ty shrugged as if he didn't care, but she knew he did. He wouldn't be asking her otherwise.

"If you don't tell me, I'll just assume it's a date."

"It's not a date."

"Is he attractive?"

"It's not a date," she snapped. "It's the chief of staff for Robertson's campaign." She deliberately left out the part about him being pleasing on the eyes. Not as pleasing as her present company, but Ty was off-limits. So off-limits he might as well be living on the moon.

Tyler frowned. "Jordan Christoff?"

"Yes. Jordan Christoff."

"Is he picking you up or meeting you there?"

"Ty." Her voice had a less playful tone to it. He didn't really have a right to ask any of these questions. They weren't a couple. They were barely even friends. They fucked. Twice. That was it. Everything else was just business.

If she weren't working for Covington things might have been different. They could have been friends. Maybe even friends with benefits. Hot, sexy, dirty, can't *catch your breath because you're drowning in orgasm*, benefits.

"I just want to make sure you're safe." Ty's words interrupted her naughty tirade. "I don't like the idea of some strange guy showing up at your door."

"And yet you keep doing that very thing."

He leaned on the counter, completely at home in her kitchen. "You know what I mean. I wouldn't be able to live with myself if something happened to you, not after the last time."

Ty didn't need to remind her of the mugging. She relived it every time she walked through an alley or an empty parking garage. She was a tough girl. Usually. But she continued to let down her guard around Tyler and it almost always ended with trouble.

"Well, you don't have to worry. Jordan is meeting me there. I'll be totally safe."

"Why don't I drive you?"

She stared at him blankly. "Are you serious?"

"Of course I am."

"You can't drive me to an event. You can't even be seen in public with me thanks to that damn photo going viral. And what if someone from the other campaign spots you? You'll blow my cover and create an even bigger scandal than the one we are trying to contain."

"You sound like Winston."

"Yeah, well maybe you should listen to him every once in a while. He knows what he's doing."

Ty reached out and took her hand. She started to jerk away but his fingers clasped down on hers and he held her in a tight grip. His lowered his head, his gaze lingering on the place where their fingers touched. She waited for him to speak, but he didn't. Instead he slowly began to caress her. His thumb massaged the base her palm. Each stroke sent a new wave of tremors through her body. He pulled her up from the couch so that they were standing mere inches apart and she could feel the burning electricity between them.

"Ty."

He shushed her with his free hand, a finger gently pressed to her lips. He locked his smoldering blue eyes on hers and she could no longer think straight.

He bent down to kiss her and she let him. His lips pressed against hers and the simple touch gave way to something more ferocious. He pressed closer to her, his arms pulling the two of them together and she felt the bulge in his pants pressing against her abdomen. The sensation sent quivers through her body. Her world began to swirl. Juliette was so dizzy with lust she didn't think she could remain standing.

Her legs gave out and the two of them fell backward onto the couch. She barely noticed the sound of ripping fabric before his weight sank on top of her, gravity forcing them together. A hand traced up her bare thigh to cup her buttocks and she thrust her hips toward him, frustrated by the heavy jeans and sequined dress in her way.

There was another tearing sound and this time it jerked Juliette back to reality.

"Shit," she cried and shoved Ty away.

Ty rolled off the couch and crashed onto the floor. The coffee table screeched forward on the wood floor and a decorative vase fell to its side.

Juliette flailed awkwardly as she tried to pull herself up without further tearing the dress.

"Don't worry, I'm all right."

Juliette ignored him. "I was going to wear this and now it's ruined."

"I think it looks good," he said, eyeing the slit in the side that rode up a few inches shy of her waist. "It's very Jennifer Lopez."

"Yeah, well I am not Jennifer Lopez." She stomped off to her bedroom and slammed the door behind her. Then twisted the lock for good measure.

The gown wasn't ruined, but it was beyond repair for the time being. Even if she could get away with the high slit on the side of the dress, there was a second horizontal tear just over her right ass cheek. Juliette pulled off the tattered remains of the red gown.

There was a knock at the door. Then a rattle of the handle.

"Go away," she said.

"I'm sorry about the dress. I'll buy you a new one."

Juliette balled up the dress in front of her, jerked the door open.

"No you will not. You will go home, Tyler. Now."

"Even pissed, you look hot."

"OMG. You are never going to get elected if you keep trying to screw every skirt that catches your eye."

She slammed the door a second time.

"You're not just another skirt," she heard Ty call from the other side. She ignored him.

"Don't dismiss what we are to each other. I wouldn't throw away a political career for just any woman."

Ugh. That was just it. He wasn't throwing away his political career. He was marrying the daughter of an incredibly powerful governor--a man who was likely to run for President in the next four years.

"Go home, Tyler," she called from the other side of the door. She listened, frozen until she heard the front door close. Then she shot across the bedroom, peeking out the window until she saw him walking down the sidewalk toward his Mercedes. Even from a distance he was sexy.

Chapter 30: False Start

She had no other choice but to wear the cream-colored dress, though it was the least attractive of the three. Maybe that was a good thing. She had her share of unwanted attention for the evening.

The gallery was close to home, on the edge of Georgetown overlooking the Potomac River. It was a small building Juliette had passed often but never bothered to visit. Personally, the art was a little too modern for her taste. It lacked the elegance and charm of the classic oils she loved so much.

The night's exhibition was no exception. She and Jordan stood in front of a ten-foot stretched canvas with a black background and several large white boxes. That was it. Nothing more. Juliette overheard someone mention how reflective it was of the modern society and our constant need to pursue the light. Juliette wanted to gag. This work wasn't good, it was lazy. And some schmuck was going to drop a couple grand on a painting she could have done in her sleep.

Juliette turned away, already bored. Until she spotted the familiar couple at the gallery entrance.

Jordan, who had his arm draped lightly around her waist, felt her stiffen and leaned into her. "Everything okay?"

"Yeah, I just have to use the ladies room." She lied. "I'll only be a moment."

She made a beeline for the bathroom before Courtney or Ty could spot her.

The moment she locked the bathroom door behind her she dialed Winston's number. After their disastrous trip through Virginia she had his cell phone on speed-dial.

"Hello, Jules."

"Don't *hello Jules* me. What the hell is he doing here?"

"By *he*, I assume you mean the senator?"

"You know exactly who I mean."

"If I had to take a guess, I'd say he's there because you're there, and I'd imagine he's jealous."

"So what? He can't be here. I can't get information from Christoff with him glaring at me from across the gallery. And Jordan Isn't supposed to know that I have any connection to the Chase campaign."

"Don't think you're telling me anything new. I said all this to Ty before he left. But the man is persistent. Once he sets his mind to something he can't be stopped."

"That's not good enough. Did he tell you he showed up at my apartment earlier?"

"He may have mentioned it."

"So why didn't you stop him?"

"I just told you the man doesn't listen to me. Not when it comes to little Ty Jr."

"Please don't use penis references with me. I don't need to hear that."

"Listen, Jules. You have the flash drive I gave you. You don't need to stay at the art gallery. Get Jordan to take you to the campaign headquarters and run the software on the drive. That's all you need to do. It will take five minutes tops."

"It's nearly 9 p.m."

"Trust me, the place Isn't deserted. And even if it is, Christoff will have a key. Get there. I'll see if I can distract Ty and Courtney."

The DNC building was dark when Juliette and Jordan arrived. They stopped in front of the odd-shaped circular building and he escorted Juliette past the main doors to a plain-looking metal door on the side. He swiped a key card, entered a code, and then pulled the glass door open. There were only two sets of elevators at the end of the hall, both of which also needed a key card for activation. Jordan swiped the plastic card and the doors slid open.

The two of them stepped inside an the elevator whisked them upwards. When the elevator stopped and the doors opened and she heard music drifting down the hall.

Winston had been right. There were people still working.

Juliette and Jordan followed the sound of Dave Mathews Band while he warned her not to take anything the guys said seriously. Then he pushed open a door and escorted her inside.

The room was as informal as the lobby had been formal. There were only a handful of offices lining the edge of the space, but the majority of the space took on an open office concept with large tables, chairs, couches, and even a small kitchenette. Like the Chase campaign offices, there was paper everywhere: flyers, posters, banners, leftover campaign materials, white boards with various numbers scrawled across every free surface. Someone had taped a piece of construction paper to the board that read, "DO NOT ERASE, or I will have your head."

Okay, so it was a little less organized than Ty's headquarters. Even with only three people, it had a chaotic energy about it.

"Jordan, you're here. I told you that art gallery was a waste of time," the redhead said without glancing up at them. The other guy gave him a nudge.

"Who's this?"

"This was my date for the evening. For some ungodly reason she wanted to learn more about the campaign, so I promised her a tour of the office."

Juliette gave a wave but before she could introduce herself properly the redhead interrupted her.

"Right, well Ben can do that. I need you now." The redhead went back to the stack of papers in front of him and the tall lanky guy grinned at her.

"No problem. I'd be happy to take this lovely lady off your hands so you two can do some real work."

Jordan apologized. "Do you mind? It will only take a minute, I'm sure." Then he left her standing near the doorway.

She followed Jordan, curious about what pressing item the two could be working on, but Ben intervened.

"So you want to see the office. I can give you the grand tour if you like. I even know some of the history of the building, if that interests you."

She shrugged. "Sure."

Getting rid of Ben was easier than she thought. When they passed Robertson's unlocked office, she faked a coughing attack and asked for a bottle of water. Then as he was leaving, she yelled to him, "I'm just going to use the bathroom. Can you set it outside the door?" And that was that. He went off, she slipped into the office, shut the door behind her, and looked out at the land mine in front of her.

Chapter 31:

Political Espionage

She set her shoes on the chair beside her. She had taken the heels off so that she could better sneak about unheard. Now she stood in front of a wall-to-wall bookshelf full of dull law review books and various accolades acclaiming his success. She moved to the plaques and skimmed them. There was a humanitarian award and another recognition from the ACLU. There were a few photos of Robertson with some rather influential leaders, including one with former President Clinton himself.

Juliette wasn't active in politics. She had never really bothered to vote, or pay attention to any election until now. For the first time since she had started this crazy adventure she questioned whether she was backing the right guy. She stared at Robertson's wall of accomplishments. He didn't seem like a monster. He seemed like the kind of person who cared about helping others.

She turned to the desk and sat down behind the computer screen. A soft green light was lit at the bottom of the monitor and she knew the computer was powered on. She jiggled the mouse and the computer whirled to life. But she was immediately greeted with a log-in screen. Crap. She didn't have time to try and figure out a password. She pulled out the flash drive from her small purse and stuck it into the USB port. Then she took out her phone and texted *READY* to the unlisted number.

The flash drive lit up and within seconds the computer log-in disappeared and was replaced with a black and white screen. Various lines of text filled the screen and she wondered if it was an automatic program running or if Winston was typing furiously on the other end. She glanced down at her phone. He was supposed to text her again when he was finished. In the meantime she could keep snooping about the office for any other intel that might give them a clue to what the Robertson campaign was up to.

She began opening and closing drawers but didn't find anything out of the ordinary. Pens and office supplies, blank stationary, and a box of cigars. Then she came to a locked file cabinet. This was something she could handle. She went back to her bag and pulled out her miniature lock-picking kit. Then she went to work. She crouched down on the floor so that she could more easily see the lock then twisted the two pieces in the metal keyhole. It took her less than thirty seconds to pop the lock.

She opened the drawer and found a handful of unlabeled file folders. The first one had a few newspaper clippings on Tyler. That wasn't surprising. Every candidate did opposition research and his appeared to be tame.

Or at least that was what she thought before she spotted the orange 9-by-11 envelope. It contained not one but several photos of Ty and Juliette. A few also contained Courtney, but those were rare. She froze when she spotted the very same picture that had run in the newspaper. So either Melissa had been trading info with the Robertson camp all along or they paid her good money to betray her friend.

What she couldn't figure out was why, if they had all these pictures of Ty and Juliette together, they didn't run more of them in the paper. Surely they recognized her as the same woman.

What if Jordan had seen these photos? Did the chief of staff recognize her as the girl with Tyler? Had her cover been blown before the night even started?

No, she cast the idea aside. She didn't recall any indication that Jordan recognized her. And he would have never taken her to the campaign office if he knew her true identity. So maybe Robertson was keeping this a secret from his team?

Jules moved to the third folder. It contained several more newspaper clippings, all related to some rezoning project. She didn't know what it was, but it looked like there was going to be a lot of money involved and the sale of some historic landmarks to private owners as a result. She flipped through the dozen or so clippings, only stopping when her eye caught a photo of Robertson at a fundraising event. There were three men in sharply dressed suits smiling back at the camera. One of them was Robertson. The other man was Senator Reis, the guy who died six months ago, after which Tyler had been appointed to fill his vacant seat.

And the last guy, she knew the face without reading the caption below. It was Dean Covington. She didn't have time to read the entire article so she snapped a couple pictures of it with her cell phone, hoping they would be clear enough to read later, and turned to the last folder in the bunch.

This one surprised her. It contained a police report for one Terrence Covington III. The name was too familiar to be a coincidence. This man, Terrence Covington, was the son of Dean Covington, her boss. Terrence, the same name of the stranger she had met in Covinton's law office, the same man who lamented with her over his father troubles at the bar down the street.

Jules stared at the mug shot in the corner of the report. The smiling face before her was one she knew well. Senator Tyler Chase.

Chapter 32: Secrets

Crap. Juliette paced the living room wondering why the world seemed to be imploding around her. How could Tyler Chase be Dean Covington's son? A devious and corrupt criminal mastermind hiding under the cloak of the law--he was the exact opposite of everything Tyler Chase stood for.

Or was he?

How much did she really know about Tyler, AKA, Terrence Covington III? Nothing, except he was criminally good in bed.

Though he had given her his real name the night they met. He introduced himself as Terrence and she had assumed the fake name was intended to keep the affair as far away as possible from his re-election campaign. But what if he was just trying to be honest?

Crap. What the hell was she supposed to do now?

Of course she knew what she needed to do--confront Ty about his past, warn him about his father, and explain the truth about what she was really doing here.

But what was she doing? Why had Dean inserted her in this mess in the first place?

Juliette grabbed her phone and dialed Ty's number before she could talk herself out of it.

He answered on the fourth ring.

"Hullo?" His voice was raspy and his breathing heavy. He sounded more than a little distracted.

She hesitated, "Is this a bad time?"

There was a muffled thud and then a curse as Ty's voice drifted away.

"Hello? Ty?"

"Sorry, I dropped the phone."

"What in the world are you doing?" It was nearing midnight and he sounded winded.

"Just getting in a workout. I had a little extra energy to burn tonight."

Code--I was too annoyed at the thought of Robertson's chief of staff groping your ass to be able to sleep tonight. See? She could read between the lines too.

And yet somehow she fell prey to the biggest scam of the century. A U.S. Senator, the son of a notorious con man, running under an entirely fake identity. *How did he manage to pull that one off?*

"Jules, you still there?"

"Yes. I'm here." Though she wasn't, not really. Her mind was reeling with unanswered questions. She couldn't even begin to figure out which to ask first.

"Did you need something?" Tyler asked.

"Oh yeah, right." *Come on, Juliette, get it together.* "I need to see you."

"Really?" His voice perked at the request.

"Don't get any thoughts. This is strictly a professional request."

"At midnight?"

'It's time sensitive."

"If that's the case, why don't you just tell me over the phone? It's d be a lot faster."

"This is something we should really do in person."

He was quiet for a moment. She pictured the frown on his face, the tight grip on the phone, the questioning look in his eyes. She was tempted to throw caution to the wind and tell him everything then and there. But he spoke again before she could work up the courage.

"I'll be there in thirty minutes," he said and hung up.

Juliette would have preferred it if they lived in a world where he could teleport instantly into her apartment. Thirty minutes was a long time for her to anxiously deliberate what she was going to say and how she was going to say it.

By the time the knock came on the door she had washed and dried the few remaining dishes in her sink and traded in the cream chiffon dress for her favorite stretchy black pants and an oversized tee. Her hair and makeup went untouched, so she imagined she looked about as frantic as she felt. Still, she pulled open the door, ready to face the issue head on.

"Oh," she let out a yelp of surprise when she saw Winston standing on the other side of the threshold. "What are you doing here?"

"We need to talk," he said. Wasn't that supposed to be her line?

"Where is Ty? He said he was coming over."

"Something else came up."

What the hell could come up that was more important than charges of fraud? Although she had to remember, she hadn't explained to Ty why she needed to speak with him. He didn't know what was going on and if Winston or Courtney came to him with another urgent matter, it was logical he would deal with the fire closest to him first.

"What is it?"

"Doesn't matter. In fact, it's better that he not be here for this. He doesn't want you involved."

Juliette stepped aside and Winston came in. He slipped off his shoes in the entryway. How considerate. Then they moved into the dining room and Winston set a hard plastic briefcase on table. It looked like something straight out of a James Bond movie. He entered in a key code and she heard the sigh of the locks releasing. When he lifted the lid she saw a top-of-the-line computer with all the bells and whistles tucked neatly into its own compartment. He clicked the built-in keyboard and the screen came to life.

"This is the info we pulled from Robertson's computer," he began.

"I know," Juliette said. "I saw some of this in his printed-off files."

"What exactly did you see?"

"Police records, background checks, photos of surveillance from everyone on the campaign. He's been following everyone for months. I don't think he was behind the mugging, but I think he is connected to someone who was."

"Like who?"

Juliette hesitated. How much did he know about Ty's father? She remembered that Winston had said he and Ty went back a long way. She couldn't imagine Ty being good enough to keep secrets from his super-hacker best friend.

"Somehow he's connected to Dean Covington."

In all the time that she had known him, Juliette had never seen Winston look shocked. It was more than a little jarring. He leaned back in the chair, forgetting all about the computer, or whatever else he had intended on telling her.

"You didn't know?"

He shook his head. "This is what you wanted to tell Ty?" he guessed.

"I thought he should know that the truth of his past might come out in the news now that the election is only a week away."

"Shit."

"Tell me about it."

Winston turned back to the computer and began to type in lines of code. After a few moments the screen changed and she saw a mirrored image of Robertson's desktop. It was still inactive. Which probably meant that everyone in the Robertson campaign was at home in bed, where she and Winston should be.

"Do you think he has copies of the information on his computer?" Winston asked.

"I don't know. I assumed that's what you came here to show me."

He shook his head. "No, I came here to tell you that your identity has been leaked."

Chapter 33:

Help From a Hacker

Juliette gaped at Winston. "My identity was leaked? What the hell does that mean?"

"It means that I got an alert fifteen minutes ago with your name in it which identified you as the girl in the photo at the motel."

"But how is that possible? No one could see my face. The people at the hotel didn't even have my name. We didn't even pay for the room we stayed in."

"Surveillance cameras."

Juliette shook her head. "No way. There were no cameras in that Podunk town. They didn't even have wireless internet or decent cell phone coverage." Besides, it was something she would have checked for before deciding to break in.

"Not at the motel," Winston said. "Cameras outside the bar where you first met. It appears that though the place is named 'Off the Record's , that's not entirely true. There's an incredible amount of security around the building."

Holy hell. She had never thought to check for cameras at the bar because she wasn't "working" then. She was off the clock. Ty should have caught it, if he was a half decent con man, but maybe he really wasn't attempting to follow in his father's footsteps.

"I'm sorry," Winston continued. "It was my fault. I secured the surveillance from the Hay Adams hotel, and they are usually so discreet about their regular clientele-- but it didn't occur to me to check outside the bar."

"So what? We didn't go into the bar together. I didn't even know him then."

"It doesn't matter. They have pictures of you two together, looking a little intimate. They know that you left together and now that they have a name, they can compare every snapshot of you they can find to the photo at the motel. They don't have to prove it is true, just report it."

Juliette wanted to scream in protest. Her name and face would be all over the internet. Major news networks would pick up the story by daybreak.

"Maybe no one will see it. You said it was just a small blog, right?"

"It's already been reposted on two larger blogs. Ty's gotten at least four calls asking for comments. If they're calling Ty, they'll be calling everyone."

"How come they're not calling me?"

"I put a block on you phone. The only calls ringing through are those verified from me."

"You hacked into my phone without asking? What the hell is wrong with you?"

"A thank you would be nice. I figured you wouldn't want to deal with a lot of pesky reporters over the next few weeks. Once the election dies down, the calls will likely go away. But for now"

A horrible thought occurred to Juliette. "How long have you been spying on me?"

"Relax, I haven't said anything to Tyler."

"How long?" she demanded.

"Since the morning I met you."

Juliette nearly knocked her chair over as she jumped up. "I cannot believe this."

"Believe it." He stood too so that his brown eyes could better meet her gaze. "And don't act so haughty. You think I was going to walk in on my candidate having a one night stand and not do everything in my power to make sure the story was contained?"

"Well you just suck." Juliette snapped. "If you were any good at your job we wouldn't be in this mess right now."

His face morphed from casual to *I just might snap your neck if you poke me with that big long stick one more time* in a half a second.

Fear bubbled up inside her. How well did she actually know Winston?

She knew that he wasn't against breaking the law to protect Ty. She knew that Ty was Dean Covington's son. She knew what Covington would do under the circumstances.

But what would Ty do? Send his "cleaner" to eliminate the evidence? He could kill her right here, in her own apartment, and eliminate any evidence of murder. They'd label it as suicide. Or natural death. No one would think twice about it.

Except maybe Mimi and Jean, who knew she was caught up in Covington's web. Now she was destined to a fate like her parents. Taken down by the very man who took their lives.

Juliette bent down to pick up her chair and tried to ignore the deadly vibes emitted her way. It took every ounce of courage in her to pull the seat upright and sit down again, but once she did, Winston's temper began to deflate. He sat down as well, but his hands were still balled into tight fists at the table.

"I should have remembered the bar surveillance." He grunted.

Juliette nodded. "Do you have a plan to contain the story?"

Winston glanced back at the computer. "It's not that easy. I can hack into one site, but not six or seven. The story is just going to keep popping up all over the net. And once the major networks get wind, it will explode."

"But if they don't have the video or the photos, the story is dead."

"If they are smart, and let's assume they are since they have held onto this information for a few months, they have the original video housed offline. Which means the only way to access the evidence is to physically destroy it. Plus we can't do anything that might look unfavorable upon the campaign. It will be obvious to anyone that the only person with something to gain from hacking the site and preventing the story from circulating is Ty. That will most definitely cost us the election."

"And the truth about Ty's father won't?"

The room was silent as the two pondered the question. It seemed unlikely. One scandal was bad enough, but they seemed to be piling on the lies faster than quicksand could swallow a flea.

"Forget about me," she said. "Let that secret play out. I slept with Ty. More than once. I'm not proud of myself and it looks bad for Ty, but he can survive that. He's not married. We can create a story that works for the campaign and paints me as the villain if necessary."

"Why would you do that?"

"Because I care about Ty. Winning this election means something to him. I don't want that ruined because of me."

"And what about you?"

"I already told you. I'm a big girl. I can take it. I may even get a few TV interviews out of it, or a book deal. It won't be the end of the world."

"It might be if you don't come through for Dean Covington. He's a dangerous man and he doesn't like to lose."

Chapter 34: Confessions

Her stomach clenched and her breath caught in her throat. That's right. He had been watching her from the very beginning. He had access to her phone. He would have seen the numbers she called. He would have known that they met at the very building where Ty's father worked.

"So you know about that?"

"Afraid so."

"Does Ty know?"

Winston shook his head. "I didn't think it was my place to tell him."

"Just like it wasn't your place to tell me that I was sleeping with my boss's son?"

"Jules, I think the reason Dean gave you the job in the first place is because you slept with Ty."

"What do you mean?"

"Let's just say Dean doesn't want Ty to succeed in the election. I think he may have set you up as a trap to distract Ty and sabotage his campaign."

Juliette laughed. "That's just silly. Why would his father deliberately use me to keep his son from winning? Wouldn't he want him to succeed?"

"Dean and his father have a rocky relationship. Ty's always trying to be something he's not. He desperately wants his father's approval, as does any man. But Dean doesn't have much faith in his son. Did you know that Ty had an older brother who died on a job in Belize?"

"No. I mean, I knew Covington had kids, but they were so rarely mentioned in my research, I assumed...I don't know what I assumed. What happened?"

"The job went bad; someone on the team betrayed them. There was a shoot-out when the police arrived and he was caught in the crosshairs." That sounded familiar.

"He was only twenty-one and good at running a con. He had a lot of his father in him. Ty's always been the second best. So imagine how hard it is to know that your father believes you to be responsible for your big brother's death."

That sounded like the Dean Covington she had grown to hate. "I had no idea."

"Like I said, it's not common knowledge. I grew up with Ty. We've been best friends since we were old enough to know what a best friend was."

It certainly explained why he was so protective of Ty. It was more than a job. He was Ty's family, his real, true family.

Juliette dropped her head into her hands. "This is all my fault. I should have known I'd make a mess of things."

"What? Don't go blaming yourself. Dean used you. That's what he does."

"I have to tell Ty. He needs to know the truth."

"No he doesn't. Despite what you think and the crazy mess we've made of this campaign, you coming into his life was the best thing that has ever happened to him. His father couldn't have predicted it; he thinks you're just another pretty distraction for his son. But I knew the moment I saw Ty follow you out of that bedroom that you were different."

"I can't just keep lying to him. Not after knowing all this."

"I'm not saying you never tell him, or that he won't find out eventually. He will. Dean will see to it. But not now. Not tonight. He can't walk away from this campaign. If he does, his father wins."

"Wins what? His pride?"

"No. We suspect Dean paid someone to assassinate Senator Reis as part of a cover-up to stall a federal investigation into his businesses."

"Wait, what?" She tried to process what he was saying.

"We got Anderson to appoint Tyler to the vacant seat in hopes that we could find enough evidence to connect Dean to the death. But so far, nothing. If Robertson gets elected and we lose the seat, we lose any leverage we have over Dean and he gets away with murder."

"It wouldn't be the first time."

"More importantly, it won't be the last."

Winston inched forward in his seat. "We have to win this election. Robertson will never stand up to a man like Dean Covington. Whatever information Senator Reis was hiding, Dean will finally have a chance to destroy it, unless we can keep him at bay."

Juliette's phone rang and she jumped at the sound. "I thought you had my calls blocked."

"Only the ones that aren't contacts in your address book."

She looked at the screen. "It's Ty."

"You should answer it."

"I can's t."

"If you don't he will assume the worst and be on your doorstep in the next ten minutes."

Winston was right. Juliette had no clue how much of the truth Ty actually suspected, but she knew he's d be worried about the news of their affair being leaked to the press. He's d want to know for himself that she was all right.

"Hello?" Her voice damn near cracked when she spoke.

"I thought you weren't going to answer. I'm sorry I haven't made it over there yet. Is Winston there? Did he tell you what happened?"

Juliette nodded her head and then remembered that he couldn't see her over the phone.

"I'm fine, Ty. Don't worry about me."

"This is a complete and total cluster fuck. Courtney is livid. She wants to personally go after any reporter who dares to air the story tomorrow."

Oh God. Courtney. She had forgotten all about her. What the hell was her role in this?

Winston waved a hand, drawing her out of her deep, dark thoughts and she struggled for something to ease Ty's worries. "I'm sure it won't look so bad in the morning. It's just a few blogs and Winston and I are working on a game plan now. He'll send you the CliffsNotes version as soon as we're finished."

"What are you talking about? We're not going to spin this. I'm going to tell the truth. I'm going to call it off with Courtney, make a public apology for my actions, and ask for forgiveness."

"No," Juliette said.

"Yes. I've already told Courtney it's over. She doesn't really believe me yet, but she will when I sit down with Barbara Walters for an exclusive."

"Please don't do this. You can't do this."

"Why not? I love you. I'm in love with you. I can't stop thinking about you. When I'm around you, it takes every ounce of my being to keep me from touching you. I want the world to know that you are the woman I love and I don't give a damn if this messes up my chance in the election."

Juliette was silent on the other end of the phone. Had he really just said those words? Did he love her? Was he willing to sacrifice everything to be with her? Winston certainly believed so. It was why he wanted her to hold off on telling Ty the truth. But if she couldn't tell him about her connection to his father, what could she do?

"Are you still there?"

"I don't love you," she said. She knew the words were a lie the moment they left her lips. "I'm sorry, Ty. But we can't be together. You need to make it right with Courtney."

Juliette bit her trembling lip and brushed away a stray tear from her cheek.

You're doing this for Ty. He needs to win this election. He needs to beat his father at his own game. And he might not love you if he knew the truth-- that you were working for his father the whole time.

"I have to go," she said. Before he could ask any more questions she clicked "end" and dropped the phone. Her hand shook as she scooted away from the table. Winston came over to her and pulled her into a strong hug.

And then, she wept.

Chapter 35:

The Disappearing Act

Juliette needed an escape. The secret identities, the lies, the looming threat of Covington slitting her throat in her sleep when he found out she abandoned her mark--it was too much to bear. She needed to get as far away as possible. She needed to leave the world of Jules Everdeen behind.

She threw on a faded sweatshirt and jeans. Then she grabbed a duffel bag from the closet and started tossing in the essentials: shirts, pants, underwear, bra, fuzzy slippers, and a cosmetics bag with small travel-size toiletries already packed. She grabbed a book from her nightstand, her keys from the counter, and a new Entertainment Weekly magazine from her stack of mail and was out the door.

Juliette didn't bother to call her godparents until she was halfway to the cabin. She had been driving the rental car for an hour and a half and was just nearing Shenandoah National Park. She pulled into a gas station to stretch her legs and dialed her parents on the cell.

"Jewel, love, it's so nice to hear your voice," Mimi crooned. "To what do I owe this surprise?"

"I'm on my way to the cabin."

Her godmother didn't miss a beat. "I see."

"I know I should have called earlier, but it was kind of a last-minute thing," she said grumpily.

"This is your home. You are welcome anytime. Day or night. You know that."

"Thanks."

"I have to say, I am a bit surprised. Is everything going well in D.C.?"

"Yeah, sure. It's great. I just wanted a little family time. It's been too long since I've been home."

"Mmm hmm." Mimi purred into the phone. She suspected Juliette of hiding something, but thankfully didn't press her over the phone. Though Juliette was certain the topic would come up more than once at the cabin. Mimi was persistent. They hung up and Juliette grabbed a Coke and gassed up. Then she was back on the road, headed to one of her favorite childhood homes.

Juliette pulled onto the gravel drive that led to her parents' cabin. The place was about as off the grid as you could get. Her parents had owned a beautiful plot of land on the edge of the Blue Ridge Mountains. In the dead center they built their dream home. With their passing it had been willed to Juliette, but over the years Mimi and Jean had adopted it as their permanent place of residence. It wasn't the typical log cabin you would expect to find in the middle of the woods, rather, a beautiful five bedroom house with three levels and an outdoor Jacuzzi and heated pool that they used in the warmer months. The living room overlooked a giant ravine that made the house feel as if it had a living landscape perched on its back wall. Juliette loved to sit on the couch and dream up adventures--all the things she would do to make her parents proud. Now as she approached the house she felt a bit of remorse for letting them down.

But her godparents didn't feel that way. They took Juliette in their arms with big hugs and lots of kisses and ushered her into her bedroom to shower and change. Then they promised a hot lunch, movies, and perhaps a game of Scrabble, a family tradition on Sunday afternoons. Though it wasn't Sunday, they seemed to let that slide.

Juliette bypassed the shower for a long bath in the soaking tub. She cranked on the water, added bubbles, and switched on the jets. Then she climbed inside and let the hot water burn away her troubles.

By the time she dried herself off, dressed, and changed she could smell Mimi's famous beignets frying in the kitchen. She quickly brushed her hair into a loose ponytail and went off to meet her family.

The food was delicious. Mimi was an excellent cook. Jean always claimed that was the true reason that he married her. But she argued it was because she was the only woman he had ever met who could smuggle the same Rembrandt painting past customs twice without getting caught.

After breakfast they filed into the living room and clicked on the TV. Jean was just getting ready to stick in a DVD when Juliette spotted the headline on the bottom of the news screen.

"Wait." She grabbed the remote and clicked to CNN, hoping she could catch the report.

There he was, Dean Covington, in handcuffs.

Juliette couldn't believe it. What the hell had gone down in the last twenty-four hours? Had Winston and Ty found what they needed to connect Dean to the murder?

The network didn't have a mug shot of Covington, though she was sure they would have sold their souls to get one. Instead they used an enlarged headshot from his corporate website. Running beside it was a video clip of him being escorted from his downtown D.C. office in handcuffs beside a frenzied looking attorney who worked in vain to shield his client from the cameras. The video faded and was replaced by another photo of Senator Tyler Chase.

"Early reports indicate that Senator Chase may somehow be connected to Mr. Covington, though at this time the FBI has refused to release any further details of their investigation."

Juliette ran to the kitchen and grabbed her phone. She hit redial without thinking as she jogged back to the living room.

She supposed she should have called Ty. But after last night she couldn't bear to speak to him. So she called Winston, the man with the plan, to ask him what the hell had happened after he left her apartment.

But Winston didn't answer and her call went straight to voicemail. She left an awkward message asking for him to call her and mentioning she wanted to know if Tyler was okay. While she was rambling, the video on CNN changed. Winston was standing in front of Tyler's private residence in Richmond, VA and a bevy of TV anchors were throwing mics in his direction.

"At this time Mr. Chase appreciates your concern. He wants to take some time to be with his loved ones as he processes this shocking news and will plan to address the press himself at a later date and time." He thanked the group and turned away, ignoring the catcalls yelled out at him, pleading for more time and information. As Winston opened the front door to the house he pulled out his cell phone from his breast pocket. Her phone began to ring before he even dialed the number.

"Winston?"

"Sorry I couldn't talk when you called. I was kind of in the middle of something."

"No, I just saw you on TV." Juliette clutched the phone tighter as she ran to the stairs and locked herself in her bedroom. "What the hell is going on?"

"I don't know. The Feds swarmed in this morning around five and arrested Dean. Somehow during that process the secret of his connection to Tyler Chase made its way to the newsroom and those news leeches latched onto it like a dog with a bone. I think a few of them suspect he is Dean's son, but they haven't found enough evidence to run it on air."

"Oh my God. Is Ty okay?"

"He's doing as well as can be expected, considering the last few hours he's had."

"Should I come over?" She offered without thinking. She was almost three hours away. Would she really just turn around and drive to Richmond just to comfort Ty? Juliette held her breath as she waited for Winston to answer.

"I'm not sure that is a good idea. He was distraught when I got here. Your declaration last night really hit him hard."

"I" She didn't know what to say. "I thought it was the right thing to do. I didn't want to become more of a distraction."

"I get that. He will too. Eventually. You should stay off the grid today. You shouldn't get any stray calls, because I'm still blocking them, but people might show up at your apartment."

"Let them. No one is home. I'm staying with my godparents and my roommate is still out in New Mexico."

"Good. I'll call you later, when I have more news."

The two of them hung up and Juliette tried to make a non-conspicuous entrance into the living room. But Jean leapt from his seat the moment he spotted her.

"How bad is it?"

Chapter 36: Daddy Issues

It took Juliette the better part of an hour to convince her godparents that she was not in any danger. They still didn't believe her, but gave up when they realized she was never going to admit to anything. "You are just like your father," Mimi muttered as she went into the kitchen to start a fresh pot of coffee.

Juliette insisted the family continue on with their day as planned so they put in the movie--Oceans Eleven, the original--and snuggled up on the couch.

When it was finished, Jean was ready to start in again, but Juliette distracted him with the request to build a fire. Then she set to a game of Scrabble on the square coffee table. They were just dividing up the letters when there was a knock on the door.

The three of them froze, and then Jean snapped into action. "Juliette, go to your room." He said it as if she were six years old.

"Père, I'm sure it's nothing."

"Now." The look on his face told her not to question his authority in his own home and she didn't really have the energy to fight him this time. She pulled herself to her feet and headed for the stairs.

Juliette knew her godfather would wait until he heard her bedroom door close before greeting the uninvited visitor. He was over-protective that way. Juliette closed her door loud enough that Jean could hear and ran to the bedroom window. She carefully peeked out from behind the curtain. Only she couldn't see anything close to the house because of the angle of her bedroom window and the slope of the roof.

She moved back to the door and pressed her ear to the wood desperate to hear anything. But she was still just as impatient as she was when she was six. She cracked the door open and tiptoed to the top of the stairs.

"I'm sorry you've come all this way. Juliette Isn't here," her godfather said. "We haven't seen her in months."

"But that's her rental car," an all too familiar voice said. Juliette raced down the stairs and was at the door before Mimi or Jean could stop her.

"What are you doing here?"

Ty was dressed in dark jeans and a black leather jacket that hung loose over his broad chest. When he looked up at her, she lost her breath. His blue eyes were so incredibly sad. As sad and miserable as she had felt.

"Look, I know you said you don't feel the same way about me, and I'm sorry to show up here unannounced--"

"Apology not accepted," her godfather interrupted. "How did you even find this place? Juliette, did you give him the address?"

"I got it from Winston. He got the info from your phone." Ty's eyes never left hers. "He told me everything," he said. "Even the stuff you didn't want me to know."

"Who is this Winston?"

"Père!" She waved a dismissive hand at him. "Can you just give us a minute?"

"Absolutely not. I am not leaving you alone with Dean Covington's son."

Both of them stared up at Jean.

"You know who this is?"

"Yes. And I know Dean Covington is a shady son of a bitch and I suspect the apple doesn't fall far from the tree."

Juliette stepped past her godfather, grabbed Ty's hand, and pulled him inside. Jean began to protest but Mimi intervened, dragging Jean off into the family room and the abandoned Scrabble game. Juliette could still hear him grumbling in the distance, but she tuned him out.

"What did Winston tell you?"

Suddenly Ty seemed nervous. He shot a quick glance around the kitchen as if scanning for bugs and then shifted back toward the door. "Look, maybe we can go somewhere private, where we can talk."

"My godfather's half deaf; he can't hear you unless he's right in front of you."

"That's not true," Jean called from the living room, though from the sound of it, he was closer than she would have liked.

Juliette stepped to the closet and grabbed her jacket. Then she opened the door and stepped out onto the front porch. Ty followed. They walked past the front garden toward the edge of the ravine in silence. After five minutes, Juliette spoke. "Are you going to tell me why you followed me out here?"

He hesitated. "Why didn't you tell me?"

"Tell you what? That I was working for your father? That I was most likely sent in to sabotage your campaign?"

"Were you? I mean, did you know?"

"All I knew was that I needed to work for Dean Covington and after I met you he offered me a job. I was supposed to become friends with Courtney."

"Why did you need to work with my father? No one works for him voluntarily."

Juliette held her breath. This was it. She could tell him the truth, or she could stick to the lie. How much did it really matter? If Dean Covington was in jail she wasn't going to get any information from him about her parents' death. But maybe, if Tyler knew the truth, he's d be able to help her find the truth.

"I think your father murdered my parents."

"Your parents were"

"My real name is Juliette Morgan. My parents were Glorianna and Archer Morgan and they were killed on a job for your father."

"And you have proof that he was behind it?"

"Not yet."

"And you thought by getting close to me I'd help you get that proof."

"No. I didn't even know you were his son! I thought I'd get on Covington's good side, that he's d trust me enough to keep me close, and I might find something useful."

"Well I could have told you that was a horrible plan. My father is a mastermind of burying secrets."

"But Isn't that what you're doing, trying to find out if he killed Senator Reis?"

Tyler kicked the grass with his foot. "I hate that man." He cast her a sad smile. "I hate what he did to you. Using you like that."

"Yeah, but he couldn't possibly know that you'd d fall for me. Even I'm not that full of myself."

"I think he's the one who leaked the surveillance video of the two of us together. I think he saw us the moment we hooked up at that bar. Why else would he deny you a job and hire you the next day?"

It sucked but she knew deep down it was likely true.

He reached out to her and she pulled away. "This doesn't change anything," she said. "Get back in your car and go home."

"I love you. I want to be with you. How many more times do I have to say it?"

"None! Because we can't be together. I can't be with the son of the man who killed my parents. I don't trust you, *Terrence*. I likely never will."

Chapter 37: Intersections

Juliette downed half a pint of Cherry Garcia ice cream and moved on to picking at a day-old batch of chocolate chip cookies. Neither of the sweets successfully chased away the guilt.

Ty came to apologize and she threw his confession back in his face. Again.

She stared down at her purse and debated whether or not to pull out her phone and call him, but Jean intervened. He scooped an arm around her shoulders and practically dragged her into the family room to watch Fight Club.

"Come on, you love Brad Pitt and Edward Norton."

She did.

An hour later Juliette made a beeline for the bathroom, scooping her purse up as she went. Once the door was closed she pulled out the cell phone and began to text Ty. She was too scared to call him; she really didn't know what to say. Plus she knew Jean and Mimi were watching her like hawks. They would hear her talking on the phone and she didn't want the extra ears.

She texted three words:

Juliette: Sorry about earlier.

She set the phone down on the counter and waited. She hoped he's d have his phone on him, that he would respond immediately and not miss her message altogether.

Thirty seconds later the phone vibrated against the bathroom vanity.

She picked it up.

Tyler: Come outside.

She read the message again. It didn't make any sense. Was he still outside in the woods where she had left him? She was pretty certain his car wasn't in the driveway.

Juliette: What? Why?

Her phone buzzed again.

Tyler: No more questions. Just come outside, now.

Juliette: I can't get out, without being spotted.

Tyler: Jules

Juliette: O.K!!! Coming.

She slipped the phone into her back pocket and noisily exited the bathroom. "I'm a little tired from everything that happened today," she called down to Jean and Mimi. "I think I'm going to call it a night. Maybe read for a few minutes and go to bed early."

Her godfather frowned at her but Mimi blew her a kiss. "Sleep tight, dear."

Juliette turned and headed for the stairs. Once she was inside her bedroom she shut and locked the door. Then she ran through the Jack and Jill bathroom, shutting and locking the door to the second bedroom. The guest room was directly over the kitchen and the window overlooked the roof of the breakfast nook. She used to sneak out at night to look at the stars. And as she got older, she snuck out to flirt with older boys. Still it had been years since she had done this, and she had been quite a bit smaller at sixteen.

What kind of con man didn't have a good escape route planned out? She was one story up, for Pete's sake. She should be able to do this in her sleep.

Juliette slipped open the window and glanced out at the roof. She grabbed onto the top ledge of the window and pulled herself up. Once seated on the sill she kicked both legs onto the roof then she slipped outside into the night sky. There was no moon, and the night was dark even with the soft glow coming from the downstairs lights. She felt her way along the rooftop, crawling slowly on her hands and knees, wishing the shingles didn't scratch at the palms of her hands like raw sandpaper.

When she reached the edge she rolled onto her stomach and grabbed onto the gutter. *Light as a feather,* she thought before she lowered her legs into the open air. Inch by inch she drifted lower, until she was fully extended over the edge and hanging from both hands. Her arms were burning. She should definitely make a trip to the gym if she wanted to pull this move again.

She let go.

Her stomach dropped as she fell to the ground. She attempted to brace her fall with some fancy twist or roll, but barely managed in an awkward crouch. Her legs tingled at the pressure but after a moment it faded and she pulled herself up.

Now she was outside. What the hell was she supposed to do?

Her butt vibrated. She nearly squealed.

Tyler: Follow the driveway out to the main road.

Juliette put the phone down and started her trek. She shivered in the wind and debated how much longer she's d be wandering around in the dark. *Why didn't you think to swipe an old sweater from the bedroom closet?*

A pair of headlights flashed on and off in the distance. She recognized the black SUV from the campaign and ran toward it. Ty rolled down the window. "Get in."

The locks clicked open and Juliette ran to the passenger side to climb in. Once she did, Ty pulled off into the darkness ahead.

"Where are we going?" she asked him.

"Somewhere we can talk."

"We already talked."

"No. You talked. Or rather you yelled. I never got my turn."

"What? I did not--" He cut her off with a hand.

"It's my turn," he said again. His voice had a touch of anger in it that left her a bit unsettled. She sank back into her seat and waited.

But when they turned onto the main road she couldn't help herself.

"Can you at least give me a hint?"

"A hint about what? Where we are going? Or what I have to say?"

"Both."

"Well, we are going to a place you have been before, and I am showing you something you've seen before, but not before I say something you have yet to hear."

"Okay." She sat back in the seat and pondered his clue. It was more like a riddle that she needed to decode. She spent summers in Virginia for years. Nothing about it was unfamiliar, so of course she had been there. That didn't narrow down the list of where they were going at all. The second part of his clue, show her something, well that covered a lot of ground too. If she had already seen it, what was the point of showing her again?

Just when she thought Tyler was going to turn and pull onto the freeway he turned onto a private dirt road. She was less familiar with this area. As they continued along she spotted a glimpse of the river between the trees and the long wooden marina that housed a small silver and navy double-decker boat. It wasn't one of those mammoth yachts that needed a small crew to operate. It was small and unassuming. Ty parked the SUV and ordered her to follow. She scrambled out behind him, still drinking in her surroundings.

"I've never been here before," she said.

"Sure you have. I remember meeting you."

Juliette froze. "What?"

"It was Fourth of July weekend. My father brought me and my brother here to escape the city. He promised we were going to have some quality time together. It turned out he had just run a job, was trying to lie low. I suspect he needed a few thousand dollars worth of jewels fenced."

"And he came to Mimi and Jean," she finished.

"Yep. He was so pleased at their work that he invited the whole family over for drinks."

"Yes, I remember now. Your mother was still alive then."

He nodded.

How could she have forgotten this? She had been obsessing over Dean for years; how could she not have remembered that he had sons? Or that she had met them?

"I remember you got sea sick. Your godparents left early when you threw up on the main deck."

"That's right. And you took the blame for me. I thought your father was going to kill you."

"I'm pretty certain the thought crossed his mind."

"How could I not have remembered this?"

"It was a long time ago. You were very young. Maybe five or six."

"Still."

"Your parents were still alive then." He took her hand. "They are the ones who got him the jewelry. Including this piece." Tyler pulled out his phone and opened a photo album.

Juliette stared at the large diamond brooch. It was the same brooch that had been on the dress she wore to the black and white charity ball.

Tyler clutched her hand.

"I think my father had something to do with your parents' death."

"Because he sent me a diamond brooch that my parents stole and my godparents fenced?"

"Because he went through the trouble of finding that brooch, buying it back and then secretly sending it to you. That's an awful lot of trouble to go through without an ulterior motive."

"He's mocking me."

"Yes, Juliette. But listen to me. I promise I will do everything I can to help you find the truth. My father has a lot of dirty secrets. One of them is bound to unravel sooner or later. If not the truth about your parents, then Senator Reis."

"Or your brother?" she said without thinking.

He let go of her hand, pulling the cell phone away from her.

"He didn't have anything to do with my brother's death."

Juliette nodded. "You're right. I'm sorry. I just" She shut up.

Tyler clearly didn't want to talk about his older brother and Juliette wasn't in the mood to push him on the subject. There had already been too many secret revelations to last her a lifetime.

"Come with me," Tyler said and led her onto the wooden dock. Their heavy footsteps echoed in the stillness of the night. When they neared the boat she remembered how large it had appeared to her as a child.

Ty stretched out a leg and stepped onto the boat before extending a hand and helping her on as well.

"I still don't understand what we're doing here. So you father is a lying, cheating scumbag. I already knew that. And yes, I met you once before, when we were kids. That doesn't change our situation now. You are a U.S. Senator. You are engaged to the daughter of the governor of Virginia. And you are in the middle of a shit-storm of controversy surrounding your true identity the minute the press finds enough evidence to avoid being sued for libel."

"I'm not engaged."

"What?" Juliette froze.

"I just thought that while you were keeping track of all the reasons why the two of us should not be a couple, you should have your facts straight. I'm not engaged."

"You called it off."

"I didn't have to. Courtney was using me as much as I was using her. My father's arrest meant we might not win the election next week, thus she dropped me like a hot potato."

"A hot potato? Do people still say that anymore?"

"Shut up. It's endearing. And it's not the point."

"Then what is?"

"I am now a very single man. But I don't intend to stay that way for long."

Tyler turned and opened the door to the main cabin. He flicked the light switch and then stepped aside, waiting for her to enter.

Juliette crossed over the threshold. The small space was glittering with twinkling lights that covered the tables, the ledges, and the low hanging ceiling above her head. The only things outnumbering the lights were the red rose petals littering the counters, tables, and floor all the way to what she guessed was a private bedroom.

Chapter 38:

Bad Intentions

"Go ahead," Ty breathed into her ear. "Make yourself comfortable." Her heart flipped in anticipation. Ty's hands on her waist seemed to be holding her up as she stepped farther into the room.

"Are you sure this is a good idea?" Her voice quivered at the mention of good.

"No." Tyler gently steered her in the direction of the bedroom. "It's a very, very bad idea. Completely and totally naughty."

Juliette's breathing quickened.

"But I have a feeling," he continued, "that you are going to want to do it over, and over, and over again."

On the third "over" she spun around in his arms so that her body was facing his. She leaned into him, desperate to feel his touch, yearning for his kiss once more.

She rose on her toes, her lips searching for his. When they met, it was as if the whole boat had been launched across the universe. She was drowning in his warm, masculine pleasure and she couldn't get enough. His hands trickled across her spine, pushing her forward, claiming her body as his own.

She staggered backward into the countertop. The dishes rattled inside. Something made of glass crashed to the floor. But neither one of them bothered to look. She wrapped her legs around his waist as he lifted her onto the counter and bent over to kiss her neck. She yanked her sweatshirt over her head, revealing the red lace bra.

"Mmm, I like it," he muttered before dipping his head lower to kiss the creamy, untouched skin of her breast. Her head swirled with each soft pluck of his lips as Tyler moved from one mound to the other and back again.

She let out a soft moan when he reached behind her to unclasp her bra. In less than a second she was completely exposed, the cool night air biting at her nipples. He rubbed his hands over her breasts, pausing at each brown nub with a flick and pull. The shock of pain sent a shiver through her stomach.

She reached for the button on his jeans and undid it with a snap. She fumbled slightly with the zipper, only because she was too distracted by Ty's tongue tracing across her shoulders to open her eyes and see what she was doing. She could feel the bulge in his pants straining against the fabric and was delighted. That stiffness was hers. She was solely responsible for his erection.

The zipper came free and she jerked his pants down with one hand. He was wearing a pair of cotton boxer briefs with an elastic waistband that proved useful when she tugged him toward her.

Suddenly she could feel him pressing against her inner thigh. Heat radiated from his groin. She tilted her hips up slightly. The tip of his penis nudged through the fly of his boxers and grazed her skin.

"I want you so bad," he muttered before reaching for her panties beneath the long denim skirt now shoved up to her waist. He stepped back long enough to slide the red panties down her bare legs, his hands caressing her hips, calves, ankles, and feet. With them off, Juliette was free to move as she pleased, completely unrestrained.

Ty didn't bother removing his pants. He simply jerked the boxers down to his knees and stepped between her parted legs.

The distance between them disappeared.

Juliette dug her fingers into his back before fingering the bottom hem of his shirt. He lifted his arms and let her pull the shirt away from his smooth chest. She tossed it to the side; it landed in the small sink. Before she could ponder if the shirt was wet, Tyler was kissing her again. His tongue massaged hers, his kiss so deep she thought he might be trying to consume her. And this time when the head of his penis brushed against her wetness she felt herself open up to him.

He hesitated only for a second. Pulling back to look down at her, those deep blue eyes drinking her in.

"Fuck me," she said and then he was inside her, one long deep thrust and she felt as if she might explode. It was better than she remembered, having him like this, with no secrets, no restraints. Her body tightened against him as he pulled backward, teasing her. She didn't want him to stop, didn't want him to pull out. She moved her hips higher in protest.

It didn't matter though, he withdrew until only the tip of him was inside her and waited, watching her, teasing her. "I don't want to rush this," he said.

"No. Now." She breathed. "Don't tease."

He pushed himself inside her again, moving deeper along her channel. The width of him filled her completely.

"Harder, or faster?" he crooned.

"Both."

Tyler pushed himself inside her once more. With each thrust he began to pick up speed, grinding and pumping into her until the two of them were banging against each other like jackhammers. More dishes fell to the floor. Her hands dug into the counter edge as she struggled to keep her balance. He slammed against her--each thrust like another declaration of his love. She cried out in a mixture of pain and pleasure as the scent of their sex filled the air. Her insides coiled tighter, ready to burst at any moment. When he exploded inside her she came undone. Her own release as epic as his.

They clung to each other, bodies drenched in sweat, their remaining clothes completely askew.

"Damn," he muttered. "It's like it gets better every time."

"I'll take that as a compliment," Juliette whispered back as he pulled out of her.

"You better, because I intend to keep doing this all night long." He set her back against the counter as he stepped fully out of his boxers and jeans. Then, standing naked in front of her, bent over to kiss her again. She felt herself rising to meet him. Greedily, ready for more.

Chapter 39:

The Hail Mary

They had sex a half dozen times over the course of the evening. They did it everywhere inside the small cabin, including the tiny shower and the cabin deck. Now they lay naked and spent on the large king bed in the lower level bedroom.

"What do we do now?" Ty played with a strand of her brown hair, twisting it around a finger and then letting it fall loose again.

"You go back to D.C. and I go back to my godparents."

"I've got a better idea. How about we both go back to your godparents?"

"No way. Jean clearly hates you, and when he finds out I snuck out of the house to be with you, he is going to hate you even more."

"Fine, then let's not go back at all. Why not just hitch this beauty to the SUV and drop it off at the nearest ocean port? We can sail south until we see palm trees and sandy beaches."

Juliette rolled on her side. "Is that what you want?"

"I want to be with you. I don't really care where we go."

"What about the campaign? Your career. Your father."

Ty grew silent.

"The whole campaign was a long shot. Winston and I thought we'd be able to find evidence of foul play on Senator Reis and connect that evidence to my father long before I'd have to run in an actual election."

"So you don't want to continue being a senator?"

"Hell no. I mean, it was fun--for a while. I thought I might actually be good at it too, but that was before I met you."

"Hey, having an affair with another woman is like a rite of passage in politics. Everyone cheats."

"Yeah, well the voters may have been willing to forgive me of that indiscretion but they won't forgive me for lying to them about my father. Who's going to elect the son of a convicted felon?"

Juliette brushed a stray hair away from his eyes and rested her palm against his cheek. She could already feel the stubble against her skin.

"Dean hasn't been convicted of anything yet. Hell, he hasn't even been charged with a crime. And if your father is as good as we know him to be, he will find a way out of this trap just like every other one that has ever been sprung on him."

"That almost makes it worse. Not only am I the son of a criminal, but I'm the son of a criminal who never gets caught. Talk about a superiority complex. If they thought I was entitled before they are going to slaughter me now."

"So you're just going to withdraw from the race? Let Robertson win?"

"What other choice do I have?"

"You can run. I mean at least try, in earnest. The people of Virginia may surprise you. And you do have a kick-ass campaign team to back you up."

"Yeah, I'm sure Winston could rig an election if he wanted to."

"No stuffing the ballot boxes," she nudged him lightly. "Win fair and square. You can do that much."

"And if I lose, what then?"

"We cross that bridge when we come to it. Ty, this is your chance to beat him at his own game. If you win, we get more time to find out what Senator Reis had on him. We get closer to finding out the truth about my parents' death. We may even live to see the day when he actually gets locked away for good."

"If I do this, I want you by my side. I'm not letting you hide in the shadows anymore."

"Don't worry about me. I can take care of myself."

He inched forward and kissed her. "You keep saying that, and I find it incredibly sexy."

She kissed him back and they gave in to another twenty minutes of *meaningless distractions.*

Showered and dressed, the two of them climbed back into Ty's SUV and headed for D.C. Juliette quickly sent a text message to her godmother, letting her know she hadn't wanted to wake them but had decided to go back to D.C. with Tyler. She emailed them the information on the rental car, hoping they would be able to return it before she got charged for an extra day. Then she and Ty worked out a new campaign strategy.

The easy part was distancing himself from his father. Since Ty had legally changed his name, he could use that as justification that he had made a clean break from his criminal father and the dirty life that he lived. He would paint a story about how he wanted to get into politics to better protect the

American people from criminals and con men like his father.

And as for his affair with Juliette, he decided to stick with a version of the truth. She would continue to use her alias, Jules Everdeen, but willingly share bits of their past wrapped in kernels of truth to keep the reporters satisfied. They would tell the story of how they had met as children and became star-crossed lovers, always bumping into each other at the wrong times. He would argue the notion that anything inappropriate ever happened while he was with Courtney. And accuse his father of working with his opponent to doctor photos out of context and mislead the public about the relationship he had with Jules.

Of course that wouldn't work on a lot of voters, particularly women who were sensitive to the notion of a cheating lover. Juliette told Ty not to worry about it. That she had an idea that might bring more women around.

By the time they hit D.C., Juliette had interviews lined up with three evening news stations and a press conference to boot. Juliette had Ty drop her off at the Georgetown metro, where he would go unnoticed by news media.

He pulled to the curb and let her out, but not before giving her a quick kiss. "See you soon."

She grinned back at him as she slid out of the car. "Count on it."

Juliette waited until Tyler pulled back into traffic, then she promptly turned and headed for the metro.

Chapter 40:

Creative Bargaining

Thanks to Winston's amazing hacking skills and constant habit of tracking people with their cell phones, Juliette knew exactly where to find Courtney. She climbed off at the Dupont Circle stop and headed for the Ritz-Carlton. She waited until she was in the building and headed for the bank of elevators before dialing Courtney's number. The phone rang as she waited.

"Hello, Jules," Courtney greeted her.

"Hi, Courtney. Do you have a moment? I was hoping we could chat."

Courtney sighed into the phone. "Not really. I'm on my way out, if you can believe that. I've been cooped up all day because of this media circus and Daddy thinks a quick trip to the spa will do me good."

"Sure it will. I think it's a great idea for you to de-stress while all this mess of a scandal dies down."

Juliette stepped into the elevator and prayed she wouldn't lose reception.

"What do you want?"

"I want to see you."

"That's not possible."

"Really. Aren't you staying at the Ritz? Room 1629?"

There was silence on the other end, long enough for Courtney to hear the ding of the elevator as it stopped on the 16th floor.

"How do you know that?" Courtney asked.

"Because Winston likes me more than he likes you, and I bring him baked goods on a regular basis. Let me in."

"No," she said. "I'm calling security."

"The moment you call anyone at the hotel I will call the press, give them your location, and invite them for an up close and personal interview with the scorned lover of Tyler chase. Hell, maybe I'll even do my own interview on your behalf. Tell them all about our torrid love triangle."

The door to the hotel room snapped open and Courtney pulled Juliette inside. "What the hell do you want from me?" she snapped as the door slammed shut.

"I want you to help get Tyler Chase elected."

"Oh please, like he stands a chance of actually winning this race."

"Riightt."

"Oh don't look at me like that. Like I'm supposed to believe you two actually have feelings for each other. You're nothing more than a dark-haired D-cup distraction. Even if he wins, he's never going to keep a girl like you on his side."

"You better hope he does," Juliette said. "Because if he does anything to piss me off I just might have to leak some stories of my own, stories about your father and his investment with Covington."

"What are you talking about?"

Juliette reached into her bag and pulled out the enlarged copies of the photos she had snapped inside Robertson's office. Photos of newspaper clippings of Governor Anderson, Dean Covington, and Senator Reis all smiling together at the ribbon cutting for the Old Post Office Pavilion.

"This doesn't prove anything."

"Oh really. So I can call a reporter up right now and let them know that your father is one of a handful of elected officials doing business with Dean Covington?"

Her eyes widened at the thought but then she scrunched up her face in anger. "You're trying to blackmail me?"

"Not trying, sweetheart. I am blackmailing you and your father both."

"For what? What do you want from me?"

"I want you and your father to release a statement to the press. I want you to tell them that you called off the engagement, not because your fiancé; was cheating on you but because *you* were cheating on *him*. Say that you fell in love with another man, and the guilt was eating you alive. You thought Tyler could take the fall when you found the surveillance photos of me and Ty, and so you lied."

"They will never buy that."

"Sure they will. You go on TV, you cry. You tell them that you couldn't go on lying to the public, that Tyler is the right man for this office and you don't want to see him punished for your mistakes."

"What if it doesn't work?"

Juliette took a step closer, the humor now gone from her face. "You better hope like hell it does."

Chapter 41: Election Day

The day of the election Juliette was a complete mess. *How did people do this, year in and year out?* Never had she been more terrified in her life. People invested so much time and money into winning an election and still on that fateful day in November it was out of their hands. They turned it over to fate and eight million people living in the state of Virginia.

They had done all that they could to make Tyler look like the better choice; still she was certain it was going to be close. Most people seemed to be eating up the many twists and turns of the campaign. Tyler caught the attention of every major news program in the country. One person had even approached them about book deals and movie rights. It was a juicy story; there was no doubt about that. But what if they lost? Would it all be worth it?

Juliette, Tyler, and Winston sat in a small closed-off bedroom at the Hay Adams hotel. Soon they would need to join the throng of reporters, politicians, and campaign volunteers awaiting them in the ballroom downstairs. But for now, until they had the final tally on which way the election would go, they waited in Ty's all-too-familiar hotel suite. Winston had set up three different monitors on the small desk in the corner and was reviewing poll counts from each major news outlet. When he wasn't looking at the screen he was on his blackberry, chatting directly with volunteers across the state. They were waiting for results in two counties. Both of them were rural and had a history of going Republican. But they had low turnout in the traditional Republican areas and Robertson hadn't gone down without a fight. If enough people were turned off by the constant scandal that seemed to follow the Tyler Chase name, it might be enough to swing the election in Robertson's direction.

Juliette wanted to drop to her knees and pray. She couldn't remember doing so in the past, at least not since her parents died and left her an orphan. But now, here she was, pacing the room with Ty, practically begging for some sort of divine intervention.

Winston froze. "Guys." He started just as the phone on the nightstand began to ring. "I think we just won the election."

Chapter 42:

Deal with the Devil

The days following the election were a blur, filled with speeches, interviews, and parties galore. Tyler and Juliette had officially come out in their relationship and were suddenly one of the hottest couples in town. Rather than ruin his campaign, the entire scandal seemed to make them ripe for any media coverage they could have dreamed of. And being in the spotlight suited them both.

Juliette curled up beneath the covers and draped a hand across Ty's chest.

"What's on the menu for today?"

"I was thinking about playing a little hooky." He lifted her hand to his lips and kissed it softly.

"I think it's a little early to start calling in sick. You haven't even been sworn in yet."

"Exactly."

Both of their cell phones began to vibrate on the nightstand. Ty ignored his and reached after Juliette when she spun to grab her own.

"Ignore it," Ty said.

She looked at the message. "It's Winston. We should answer it. It might be important."

"Whatever it is, I promise it can wait ten minutes."

"Ten minutes? Is that all I'm worth now?"

He smacked her ass. "Damn straight."

Juliette ignored him and dialed Winston's number. He answered after the first ring. "What's up?"

"Is Ty with you?"

"Of course he is."

"Good. Put me on speakerphone."

"All right, but I can't guarantee he'll listen. He seems to be in an ornery mood this morning."

"He will want to hear this," Winston said and Juliette stiffened.

Ty's hand stopped caressing the curve of her thigh. "What is it?"

Juliette put Winston on speakerphone and set the phone between them.

"I just hired your new chief of staff."

"Excuse me?" Ty said.

"Wait, I thought you were his chief of staff."

"Nah, it's not a job I want. My goal was to get him elected. I did that. But I don't want to be tied down. I work better off the field, under the radar, so to speak."

"So then who did you hire?" she asked. Juliette had never given it much thought. Winston had always seemed the perfect choice.

"Courtney Anderson."

"What?" Juliette and Ty exclaimed at the same time. Winston waited as they hurled a flurry of questions and curses his way. Tyler had jumped out of the bed and was stalking around the room half naked as he argued with an invisible Winston. Finally, Juliette picked up the phone and cut Ty's rant off.

"Why?"

"Because we owe her. And she'll be good at the job. And did I mention we owe her?"

"What makes you think she'll even take the job?"

"She already told me yes."

"You asked her without even consulting me! You can't fucking do that!"

"Jules," Winston pleaded softly on the other end of the line.

"Relax. I'll work on Ty, if you really think this is the right decision to make."

"I do. We owe her," he said again. Juliette nodded though no one was in the room to see her. Ty had stomped into the bathroom and she could already hear the shower running. Winston hung up and Juliette clutched the phone to her chest as she fell back into the pillows.

What in the world had he gotten them into?

Thank you fore reading Dirty Little Liars. If you enjoyed this book please consider taking a moment to rate and/or review the book on Amazon.com, BN.com or on iTunes.

Visit the Missy Lynn Ryan website to subscribe to the official Missy Lynn Ryan Newsletter and receive a FREE short story featuring Tyler and Juliette.

About the Author

Missy Lynn Ryan is the author of the contemporary romance series Dirty Little Liars. A lover of whimsy and magic she has been telling stories (mostly ones of fiction) since she was able to string together her first sentences. Missy currently lives in the Midwest and is a current graduate student in the Seton Hill Writing Popular Fiction Program. She looks forward to the day when she can relocate to the sunny beaches of the south and spend her days writing in the sand.

Visit Missy Lynn's website at:
http://www.missylynnryan.webs.com
Join Missy Lynn on Facebook at:
http://www.facebook.com/missylynnryan
Follow Missy Lynn on Twitter at:
http://twitter.com/missylynnryan

www.ingramcontent.com/pod-product-compliance
Lightning Source LLC
Chambersburg PA
CBHW051427170626
46809CB00006B/2352